THE ROAD HOME

The Route Home: Book 2

JENNIFER CROSSWHITE

Tandem Services Press

SOUTHERN CALIFORNIA

Praise for Jennifer Crosswhite

What Readers Are Saying…

"Definitely on my to-buy list now. I can't wait for more!"
Hawaiibooklover, Amazon reviewer

"I look forward to reading more of [her] books." Amazon
reviewer

"If you enjoy a good, clean love story then give this novella a try.
You will not be disappointed." Danielle, Amazon reviewer

Other books by Jennifer Crosswhite

The Route Home series
Be Mine, prequel novella
Coming Home, book 1
The Road Home, book 2
Finally Home, book 3

Contemporary romance
The Inn at Cherry Blossom Lane

Hometown Heroes series, writing as JL Crosswhite
Promise Me, prequel novella
Protective Custody, book 1
Flash Point, book 2
Special Assignment, book 3

In the Shadow series, writing as JL Crosswhite
Off the Map, book 1
Out of Range, book 2
Over Her Head, book 3

Eat the Elephant: How to Write (and Finish!) Your Book One Bite at a Time, writing as Jen Crosswhite

Devotional
Worthy to Write: Blank pages tying your stomach in knots? 30 prayers to tackle that fear!

To my grandpa, Roy Crosswhite, who would have liked the hero of this story. Like Josh, Grandpa could build anything and liked a good Western. No family gathering is complete without at least one Grandpa story. See you soon, Grandpa!

And be ye kind one to another, tenderhearted, forgiving one another, even as God for Christ's sake hath forgiven you.

~Ephesians 4:32

Chapter One

PORTLAND, OREGON ~ SEPTEMBER 1881

The wind pushed up white-tipped waves on the water and bent the limbs of the trees lining the Columbia River shoreline. Dark clouds piled up to the south, directly in the path of the ferry Emily Stanton rode. She paced along the railing of the ferry, tapping her gloved fingers on the top rail, glancing at the ominous clouds. Up the Columbia, down the Willamette, and soon she'd be in Portland. The rhythmic slapping of the sternwheeler's paddles on the water echoed her restlessness. She turned to pace again—her long strides hampered by her narrow-heeled boots—as if her movement would hurry the boat. Turning again, she nearly collided into a man sporting a shiny mustache that matched the coal black of his eyes.

He grabbed her arm to steady her, his fingers grasping her arm a little too tightly through her wool sleeve.

His cologne overwhelmed her. Pulling her head back slightly, she took shallow breaths through parted lips. "Excuse me. I didn't see you."

"That's quite all right." He still held her arm, his eyes like dark pebbles.

A shiver ran up her spine. While he dressed like a gentlemen, her instincts convinced her he wasn't. Considering those instincts had saved her more times than she could count, she pulled away.

He tightened his hold.

"Where are you goin' in such a hurry?" His mouth twisted in a too-friendly smile.

She pressed her lips into a firm line. "I said, excuse me." She tugged her arm harder, managing to free herself from his grasp. She attempted to brush past him, but he blocked her way.

"No need to get uppity. Just tryin' to be friendly. No harm in that, right?"

Emily spun and walked the other way. The man's low chuckle followed. Leaving the promenade, she strolled inside the enclosed area of the superstructure. She spotted a seat near an older couple, but she wanted to be left alone and not forced to make polite conversation. There was too much on her mind. She needed her book so she wouldn't be bothered.

Threading her way through passengers and cargo, she reached her valise. Tucked into a corner, it sat nearly hidden next to a few other bags. She snapped open the faded, threadbare carpetbag to retrieve a book, but her fingers touched a smooth, hard edge. Sliding it out, she studied the eyes in the tintype. *Thomas.* Lightly tracing the face she whispered, "Soon. I'll be home soon." She gazed at the photograph a moment longer before pushing it farther back into the bag. Snatching the book she originally came for, she clicked her bag shut.

Making her way back to the couple, she sat next to them on the leather bench and, after a polite nod in their direction, buried herself in the story. Secure behind her book, her thoughts wanted to wander, but she reined them in, forcing herself to concentrate on the words on the page, knowing it was the fastest way to make the time pass.

Emily soon lost herself in the pages. The steam whistle blew a seemingly few moments later, startling her. She was here. Her stomach quivered.

The crew called to the passengers to gather their belongings. Closing her book, she retrieved her valise. The catch was unlatched, so she stuffed her book back inside and carefully latched it. It wouldn't do to have her bag come flying open when it got tossed onto the stagecoach.

A slight bump signaled the ferry had moored at the Alder Street wharf, and passengers lined up to cross the lowered bow ramp. After standing in one spot for several minutes, swaying with the movement of the ferry, Emily wondered why no one was moving. She was tired, her valise as heavy as if it were filled with lead. She shifted her weight and switched the bag to her other hand, tapping her fingers on the railing.

Looking around, Emily smiled. This was one time her height gave her an advantage, allowing her to spot the cause of the delay. At the end of the bow ramp, a man questioned each person as they disembarked. She watched as he stopped the men and asked to look through their bags. When he shifted, the sun glinted off his badge.

A frisson of fear weakened her limbs. She took an even breath and reminded herself that she was a new creation in Christ. Old things were passed away, and she had no reason to fear.

But old habits died hard.

Emily heard some murmurings among the passengers. Finally, one stopped a crew member hurrying by. "What's going on?"

The burly man halted mid-stride. "A payroll delivery got held up a few days back, and the sheriff seems to think the robber might be on this ferry."

Passengers' voices grew louder. A man several people in front of Emily wondered aloud who the robber was and if he'd conversed with him on the trip.

Emily's heart beat a little faster. She studied the sheriff.

Another man wearing a different type of badge stood near him. Portland's marshal, she assumed. The two men would occasionally look at a piece of paper the sheriff held as each man passed by.

Taking a few even breaths, she distracted herself by looking around. A bit behind her, a father was boosting his little girl up in his arms so she could look over the railing and out into the city. Her curls were caught up in a bow and her dress cascaded over his arm. He whispered in his daughter's ear, and she giggled and squirmed. The mother, slightly behind them, smiled.

Emily's heart squeezed. A family. Something she'd never really had. But with Thomas, maybe someday that would be possible. If the Lord allowed it. And she desperately hoped He would.

Blinking and looking away, she inched her way down to the bow ramp with the rest of the passengers. Ahead she noticed the man she'd run into earlier. He was fingering his collar and shifting his weight from foot to foot. No doubt thinking he had somewhere important to be. As if the rest of them could just stand there all day.

It was the man's turn, and the sheriff and marshal looked repeatedly at the paper they held while questioning him. Their voices were low, and the wind coming off the river caught their words before Emily could hear them. They examined the man's bag more thoroughly than anyone else's and reluctantly, it seemed, sent him on his way. She smirked at his obvious relief and hoped he was late to wherever he needed to be.

The officers moved quickly through the rest of the line. In no time, she found herself walking down muddy Front Street to the horse-drawn streetcar. It would make quick work of the ten blocks to the Oregon Express stage line office, the last leg of her journey home. And to the start of her dreams finally coming true.

She hoped.

Josh Benson headed down the street in Portland toward the Oregon Express stage office to see if there were any passengers for tomorrow. Given the dark clouds piling up overhead, he almost hoped not. The fire just two months ago had scorched the earth along much of the road to Reedsville, meaning a soaking rain was likely to cause a mudslide.

On the other hand, no passengers wasn't good news either. With the Oregon Express mortgaged to the hilt, he had to have fares coming in to make the payments. This was why he had always hated the bondage of debt. But it had saved his best friend's logging company, and he would do it again as sure as his heart beat.

As he blew out a breath, a reflection in the hardware store window caught his eye. A new display of woodworking tools and a deluxe tool chest with a hinged lid and lined, compartmented drawers with brass latches. Pa had had one like that before Josh had to sell it to pay for Ma's medicines. Not that the medicines had helped. His hands tingled as he examined the tools, imagining their heft and smooth weight. The sharp chisels would cut through wood like butter.

He shook his head. Someday he'd have time for more woodworking, but not until the Express was back on solid financial footing.

The glass shimmered, reflecting movement on the street behind Josh. He studied the window.

Not today. Lord, I just can't talk to him today.

It was as if his memories had conjured up his father and set him on the street. Without turning around, Josh picked up the pace and headed toward the Express office, hoping he could figure out a way to dodge Pa before Pa caught up to him.

EMILY HURRIED DOWN the boardwalk in Portland toward Josh Benson. The last light of the day danced off his brown curls as he strode out the barn behind the stagecoach office whistling.

Recognition flickered in his eyes. "Emily!" He closed the last few steps between them. "How are you?" His grin caused the dimples she remembered so well to dent his cheeks.

Pleasure warmed her throughout, surprising her in its intensity. Dropping her valise at her feet, she smiled. He was tall. So much so she actually had to tilt her head a bit to meet his gaze. Usually she was at eye level or above most men. "I'm well. It's good to see you again."

"So has your grandfather recovered?"

Grandfather. Emily's chest constricted. Ever since she'd known the truth, she couldn't bring herself to call the man that, but she couldn't tell anyone else.

"Uh, yes, he's better. He had the grippe, and his recovery was longer than expected. But he's back on his feet." Doing what he did best.

"Are you coming back to Reedsville to teach?" Josh asked.

She hesitated. Married women couldn't teach, so if she took Thomas up on his proposal, she wouldn't be teaching for long. "Yes, for now." She'd been gone so long, she wasn't sure the school board hadn't replaced her with another teacher yet, especially considering the term should be starting any day.

He nodded. "That's great. The town has really missed you."

Her pulse quickened. Had Thomas missed her too? She was so close. "When's the next stage to Reedsville?" She struggled to keep her voice calm, but she was sure Josh heard it crack.

He crossed his arms. "It normally would be tomorrow, but those clouds—" he motioned behind him toward the mountains with a jerk of his head—"have been dark and threatening since yesterday. I suspect it's been raining there pretty steadily today. I'm not sure the roads are in good condition. We had a big fire last summer, and the roads are washing out with any amount of rain. Since I don't have any passengers here, I was thinking of waiting a couple of days."

"Oh." She swallowed. "I was hoping you could take me to Reedsville tomorrow."

He was silent for so long, disappointment welled up. She worked to keep her lips tilted up as they wanted to slip down. She'd been gone nine months. A few more days wouldn't matter. Still, she'd hoped.

He shifted his weight then glanced around. "Okay. We'll leave in the morning. But be prepared to be cold and wet."

She wasn't sure she'd heard him correctly. Then her heart rose in her chest. "What? Oh, yes. Thank you so much. I really appreciate it."

Josh grinned. "I'd like to get home too. Staying in the city too long makes me antsy."

She twirled a loose curl at her neck. "What time should I be ready to leave in the morning?"

He stared down the street. The moment stretched. Was he going to answer her? "Do you have a place to stay? Because I think Josiah Blake would be happy to share supper with us, and I think Mrs. Hanson could find a bed for you."

She had forgotten how kind Josh could be, especially since his kindness was often covered with humor. A meal with an old friend and a bed at her former employer's hotel felt as much like coming home as anything she could remember. She cleared her throat. "That sounds lovely."

With another quick glance behind them, Josh snatched up her valise and offered his arm. "Shall we?"

For once, she was glad for her long legs allowing her to keep up with the brisk pace he set. Whatever his hurry was, she wasn't about to ask. He was taking her to Reedsville, and that was the important thing.

She didn't want to push her luck.

EMILY HEFTED her valise onto the bed Mrs. Hanson had found for her. The valise still felt heavy but maybe she was just tired. A good night's rest should be the cure.

Today had been more moving than she had expected. Mrs. Hanson had greeted her with a warm hug and an offer of employment. Josiah had been the courtly gentleman she'd always known him to be, the elder image of his son, Seth Blake. And Josh had been as comfortable and familiar as an old friend and seemed genuinely glad to see her. Supper had been warm, filling, and full of delightful conversation. She felt… at home.

And she hadn't even been reunited with Thomas yet.

She unpacked her nightgown. *Thomas.* She hadn't heard from him in six months. Not that she expected to the way she'd left things. Still, she'd hoped.

What would he say when he saw her again? Had his feelings changed? Would he be angry with her? There was no way to know before she arrived. Unless she asked Josh.

No. She discarded that idea immediately. What could she possibly ask him? She'd worry about it when she arrived. No purpose in stewing about it now.

She sighed and reached in her bag for her book. Perhaps reading would get her mind off things and help her settle down to sleep. She dug around, trying to find her book, when her fingers brushed soft leather.

"Oh no." She groaned. "Not my work boots." Expecting to pull out a pair of boots ruined by the damp, she grasped the leather and yanked.

She gaped. It wasn't her boots. It was a soft leather pouch, bulky and fairly heavy.

Confusion swirled through her brain as her fingers fumbled with the leather tie, and she opened the bag. What was it, and how did it get in her valise? Peering inside, she saw what looked like paper. She withdrew a bundle and blinked, not believing what she was seeing: bank notes, issued by the National Bank of Walla Walla.

Her hands shook as her mind put the pieces together. She flipped through the bundles of tens, fifties, and even some hundreds, quickly totaling several thousand dollars. Her supper threatened to come back up. *Silas, how could you?* He'd promised he'd changed!

She sank on the bed, the money quivering in her hands. He must have slipped it in her bag before she left Seattle. Why had he done this? But she knew why. He was trying to take care of her. He never believed her when she told him she didn't need his help.

Angry tears welled as she clapped her hand over her mouth to stifle a sob. Her shoulders shook as she rocked on the bed, tears streaming down her face.

Silas was going to ruin everything, everything she'd worked so hard for. If the townsfolk found out, if Thomas found out…

She took a deep breath and another, getting her emotions under control. When the tears stopped, she wiped her eyes with the backs of her hands and forced the painful thoughts from her mind. Pushing herself off the bed, she moved to the washstand and splashed water on her face. She glanced back. The leather pouch on the bed seemed to accuse her, mock her, tell her she hadn't changed.

"I have changed," she whispered through gritted teeth, fists clenched at her side. "I know I have, even if Silas doesn't." Hadn't Mrs. Luke told her she was a new creation in Christ? She never failed to include those words in each of her letters.

Emily reached for her valise where the latest letter from Mrs. Luke was ensconced. Maybe reading the words would reassure her.

But to prove she had changed meant one thing. Despite the awful dread in her stomach, she knew she had to get the money back to its owner.

She plopped back on the bed, letter folded in her hand. Now what? She should go back to Seattle and confront Silas. Make him give the money back. But how would she explain that to

Josh. "Oh, I do apologize, but I'm afraid I've changed my mind" wouldn't be enough after she'd begged him to take her to Reedsville. And if the rain that had started falling while they were at supper washed out the road as Josh had feared, she might not be able to return to Reedsville until the roads dried out. Her teaching job would most definitely be gone by then.

She slapped her hand on the bed. *Silas, why do you keep ruining my life?*

What if she took the money to the marshal's office in the morning? He probably wouldn't believe she'd happened to find the money in her valise. She would have to explain about Silas. There'd be a lot of questions, and she'd delay Josh. Assuming the marshal would even let her go.

Silas would most likely end up in jail. While he continued to make her life difficult, he had raised and provided for her for many years. Such as it was. While it wasn't the most honorable way to grow up, it could have been worse. Far worse. She had seen what had happened to other children forced to live on the streets. For that, she owed him something. At least the chance to make things right himself.

A knock at the door sent her heart racing. Had they found her already? She swallowed twice before she could find her voice. But as she opened her mouth, a familiar voice came through the door.

"It's Mrs. Hanson. I just came to say goodnight."

Emily returned the letter to her bag and flung open the door.

Mrs. Hanson's eyes widened. "Oh my dear girl." She moved over to the bed and patted a spot next to her.

Emily swiped at her cheeks, embarrassed to find them damp. Her face must be blotchy too. How would she explain it? She sat next to Mrs. Hanson and was immediately enveloped in a warm hug.

"It's okay, just let it all out. We've had our time to grieve. Now it's your time."

Emily's mind reeled trying to catch up with Mrs. Hanson. What was she talking about? Or rather, who?

"It might be hard, but going back to Reedsville and being among folk who are practically family to you will help. You'll see."

Emily nodded. That was something she could agree with. With a final sniff, she pasted on a tremulous smile and pulled back. "Thank you. You're very kind." No further enlightened as to whom Mrs. Hanson was talking about, Emily was nevertheless grateful for the misunderstanding that kept her secret a secret.

Another quick hug and Mrs. Hanson was out the door.

Emily quickly changed into her nightgown and crawled under the covers. Thoughts firmly back on her original problem, she wasn't going to let Silas derail her plans any longer. She was going to see Thomas. Then she'd write Silas and get the money back to its rightful owner.

Somewhat satisfied by her decision, she tried to read, but she couldn't seem to concentrate on the words. She put down the book and blew out the lamp. Trying to focus her thought on pleasant things, she thought about her reunion with Thomas and what the future might look like for them. He might present a complication in her getting the money back to Silas.

The thought emerged that maybe she could tell him. Tell him everything, and not just about the money. He was a kind and fair man. He would understand.

Wouldn't he?

She couldn't risk it. The last time she had trusted someone with her secret, it had nearly ruined her life. Once she and Thomas were married, her past wouldn't matter. Everything would be fine, just as she planned.

But after wrestling with the covers for hours, sleep wouldn't come. Her mind drifted, wondering who Mrs. Hanson was talking about.

Chapter Two

It still drizzled heavily the next morning. Josh figured he'd be soaking wet the rest of the day. His oilcloth duster would only work so well. But he'd known that would be the case when he agreed to take Emily to Reedsville. He wasn't afraid of the rain, even if the arm he broke last summer ached a bit. Entering the Oregon Express office, he grabbed a tin cup off the shelf above the pot-bellied stove sitting in the center of the small room. He poured coffee from the pot he'd started before caring for the horses. It'd warm him up for the time being.

He replayed the stretch of road that had burned that summer. And considered how much rain had already fallen and how much might still fall before they got to Reedsville. He glanced around the waiting room as he sipped. Empty. No passengers. Which was not good news for his bottom line. If it weren't for Emily, he wouldn't even make the run.

He grimaced as he swallowed the last of the brew. She gave him an excuse not to call himself a coward. If he had to stay in Portland, he'd either have to continue avoiding Pa or actually talk to him. He'd tackle a mudslide any day over that.

The door opened, and Emily entered, dropping her bag at

her feet and shaking the damp off her hands. "Good morning. Glad to see you didn't leave without me."

"Morning. You're early. And my only passenger." He reached for another cup. "Coffee? We'll be here a few more minutes."

Emily nodded. "I think these will go well with coffee." She unwrapped a cloth-covered bundle.

The smell of yeast and cinnamon wafted his way. "Mrs. Hanson's famous cinnamon rolls." He grabbed one and took a bite. One of the best things he'd ever tasted.

Emily grinned. "I figured it would help sustain us during the bad weather."

Josh popped the rest of the roll in his mouth and chewed while he poured a cup of coffee and handed it to Emily.

She wrapped both hands around the mug. If she was cold now, it was going to be a long day.

"I'll get the mail loaded and bring the coach around. Then we'll be off." He snatched up the satchel of mail from behind the counter and headed out the back door to the barn, hurrying so the mail sack didn't get too wet. He pushed open the barn door, lifted the cover of the boot on the stage, and heaved the mail sack in.

He was glad he was driving this stage run instead of James. He figured they had an even chance of some part of the road being too muddy to cross. Plus, he'd promised Emily. After her being away so long, the least he could do was get her to town as soon as he could.

Last night had been one of the more enjoyable ones he'd spent in recent history. He'd tossed out the invitation to Josiah Blake's on the spur of the moment. He'd seen Pa rounding the corner of an alley behind them. He didn't want to talk to Pa, especially not in front of Emily. She didn't know about his past, and she didn't need to. Josiah would welcome them any time for supper, and Pa wouldn't darken Josiah's door. Pa was too ashamed to be around Josiah, the man who had raised Josh alongside his own son, Seth, since Pa wasn't capable. Or willing. Josh still wasn't sure which.

He pulled down the tack and began harnessing the horses. He'd known Emily from when she was teaching in Reedsville, and before that when she'd worked for Mrs. Hanson at the hotel. But when he saw her yesterday, she seemed different somehow. He'd never noticed her eyes were the same grey-blue as the ocean or how her pale blonde hair caught the sunlight. For the first time, he saw her as a woman and not just some girl he'd known forever.

Of course he'd always thought she and Thomas would get married. He didn't know what had gone on between them. Thomas sure never let on about it. But they had spent a bit of time together and no one, not even him, could miss the looks they sent each other's way. Thomas was supposed to have been writing her when she left—

He stopped, resting his hand on the horse's muzzle. She didn't know about Thomas. He was sure no one had thought to write her. If they'd even known where to reach her.

He stared at the barn door, his stomach dropping to his boots. He did not want to be the one to tell her. He wasn't good at that stuff. That was Maggie's job. She was the motherly type. He didn't know how to deal with tears. The weather would be bad enough. He didn't think he could handle her crying all the way to Reedsville.

He tightened the harness and started on the next horse while deciding what to do. Would it be fair to let her ride the whole trip thinking she'd see Thomas at the end of it? Would it be cruel to let her find out after she arrived? If he told her now, would she change her mind about going?

No, she was the schoolteacher. She had to come back for that. Plus, he didn't want to let her sit in the stagecoach to grieve all by herself with no one to comfort her. It would be better for her to find out in Reedsville with Maggie and Becca around to console her. It would be better for him, too, but he didn't dwell on that angle too long.

Stagecoach hitched up and ready to go, he brought it around front, hopped down from the driver's seat, and strode into the office. Picking up their bags, he avoided her eyes. "Ready?"

Her gaze darted up, and she stopped pacing the floor. "Yes." She followed him out the door, closing it behind them, remaining under the covered part of the sidewalk.

He carried their bags to the stagecoach, glancing back over his shoulder, hoping she couldn't discern he was hiding something.

She was watching him and opened her mouth as if she were going to speak.

He paused. If she asked how Thomas was, he had to tell her.

But she closed her mouth without saying a word.

He repressed a sigh of relief as he stowed their bags in the boot.

Walking carefully around the stagecoach, he checked it, the horses, and the lines one more time. Water sluiced down his neck every time he leaned over, but he ignored it as best he could. Making sure the boot was fastened, he opened the stagecoach door.

Emily had been apparently lost in thought; it was a moment before she noticed the open door and hurried over.

He gave her little help as she leaped into the stage.

With a murmured "thank you," she perched on the coach's cushions. He closed the door and climbed up to the driver's seat. Shouting to the horses, he slapped the reins across their backs and they were off. Whether or not he had done the right thing. . . Well, he had the whole ride to debate with himself.

THE DRIZZLE steadily increased to rain as they headed south. Josh was thoroughly soaked and cold to the bone by the time they reached the boardinghouse the Oregon Express had contracted to serve their noon meals. He was looking forward to some hot food and hotter coffee.

Josh spotted the mistress of the way station, Mrs. Vandermeer, step onto the porch as they pulled up. She would be surprised to see them in this weather.

Mrs. Vandermeer looked up at Josh. "Well, you go take care of them horses, and I'll have hot soup and dry towels for you when you come in."

"I'd truly appreciate that."

She helped Emily out of the stage and hurried her inside.

Josh pulled the stagecoach around to the barn. The cold made his arm stiff as he hurried to take care of the horses, but moving quickly helped him warm up. Mrs. Vandermeer's son, William, was an able assistant and they made quick work of it. A short time later when he stepped inside, Mrs. Vandermeer had dry towels ready for him.

He and Emily exchanged few words while they ate. He hoped she wouldn't ask about Thomas, so he hesitated to bring up anyone in Reedsville in case it might lead to that.

Emily divided her glances between her food and the windows, as if she was expecting someone. Quite different from the woman who had been enjoyable company at supper last night. But who could understand women?

As much as he dreaded going back out into the wet and cold, they had to get moving if they had any chance at getting to Reedsville before the road washed out. As soon as Emily had finished, they thanked Mrs. Vandermeer and hurried out to the stagecoach.

Emily studied Josh and then the stagecoach. "Could you make sure our bags are still in the back?"

He frowned. That was an odd request. "Sure. Never had anyone bother anything back there before. It's not like we're carrying payroll or anything." He unfastened the boot and looked in before lifting it higher for her to see. "Everything's still there." He smiled, hoping she was reassured. What had gotten her so agitated?

She nodded and continued to the stagecoach door.

He helped her in, not knowing what to make of her. Yesterday, she'd seemed happy and eager. Now she seemed worried or fearful—he couldn't decide which. He checked the oilskin flaps covering the stagecoach windows, making sure they were still securely fastened. Whatever it was, something was bothering her. Even he could see it.

Was she nervous, thinking she was going to see Thomas again? As he climbed up to the driver's seat, a pang of guilt shot through him. Too late to do anything about it now. All he could do was get them both to Reedsville as soon as possible.

JOSH HUNCHED over the ribbons woven through his fingers with just the right tension. Years of practice allowed him to guide the horses while studying the road intently through a thickening curtain of rain. They might just make it. Outside of town, the road dropped steeply and snaked along the edge of a gorge. There was nothing to keep the soil from washing away.

Rivulets of muddy water surged down the mountain, gouging the soil. A sinking feeling roiled Josh's gut. Instinctively, the team slackened their pace. He leaned forward to peer through the rain.

Vibrations shook him before he heard the first rumble. His hands reacted instinctively, jerking back on the ribbons as the horrifying roar of a mudslide reached his ears.

The horses needed no encouragement. They stopped in their tracks. A split second later a wall of mud, rock, and charred logs tumbled down the hillside and spilled across the road. He could only watch and hope the slide didn't reach them. The lead and wheel horses tossed their heads and shifted their weight, trying to escape the danger they sensed. He held the ribbons firm.

"Please, Lord, keep us safe." Frozen to his seat, he watched fingers of the slurry reach toward them, unable to do a thing to stop it or save them. Imperceptibly, the rushing ooze lost speed. He had to blink and rub his eyes. A moment later he knew it was true, and soon the sludge merely crawled along, stopping just short of them.

Breathing a prayer of thanks, he wrapped the ribbons around the brake and hopped down. Going down the line, he patted each of the horses and praised them. Satisfied they were fine for the moment, he headed back to the stagecoach and opened the door.

Emily gripped the seat, her face paler than usual and her eyes wide.

"A mudslide washed out the road. We can't go any further."

"Is that what that noise was?"

Josh nodded.

"Are we going to be all right?"

"Sure." At least he hoped so.

INSIDE THE STAGECOACH, damp cold oozed into Emily's bones. She wrapped her arms tighter around herself. Sounds of Josh sloshing around outside unhooking the horses from the stagecoach competed with the steady drumming of rain on the roof.

If she were moving around, she'd have a better chance at staying warm. Though getting wet would make her colder.

The stagecoach door opened, and Josh stuck his head in, water from his hat dripping on the floor. "I've got the horses unhitched and the mailbag situated. Have you ever ridden bareback before?"

Her limbs turned liquid, and her pulse throbbed. With all

the noise Josh was making outside, she assumed he had a plan. Just not this plan.

She didn't like horses. Correction, she was terrified of horses.

She shook her head. She tried to speak but had to swallow to dislodge the knot in her throat. "No, but I don't have much of a choice now, so I suppose I'll manage." She'd done many things that were distasteful, and even things that had terrified her. But that didn't mean she liked it.

"The sooner we get headed back the better." He extended his hand.

She stared at his hand. Shoving away the up-swell of fear, she grabbed his hand, feeling the dampness on his gloves seep through hers. She had no choice but to trust him.

On shaking legs, she stepped from the coach, and promptly sank up to her ankle in mud. Her small, fashionable flowerpot hat did little to protect her from the rain that now trickled down her neck. Repressing a groan, she attempted to take a step, only to find that she couldn't. The mire clung tightly to her and threatened to steal her boots from her feet.

Josh grasped her hand tighter, giving her the resistance she needed to pull her foot free.

Reaching the horses, her fear rose again. She concentrated on breathing evenly but couldn't quite get the fear to back down. These horses were huge. They hadn't seemed so large when hitched to the stagecoach. How did Josh think she could climb on one, let alone ride it? With a toss of its giant head, it could fling her into a pile of bones.

She turned. "I—"

"Here, I'll give you a leg up." He knelt and laced his fingers together, forming a place for her to put her foot. The horse shifted its weight, looming larger. She squealed and grabbed Josh's shoulder.

He squinted up at her, rain pelting him in the face. "It's okay, Emily. Trust me. I won't let you get hurt." Damp, dark lashes framed his eyes, making him look like a little boy.

She cast around for some other option. This was it. There was no other alternative. This was the only way. She squeezed her eyes shut and sent up a quick prayer for safety. Then she put her foot in Josh's hand, grabbing his shoulder instinctively for balance.

"Grab the mane!" In the next moment she was flying through the air. She was so startled it took a moment to remember the purpose was to get on the horse. She groped madly for the mane that slipped through her fingers. Getting a fistful of horsehair flooded her with relief. Instantly replaced by her ribs colliding with the horse's back, knocking the wind out of her.

She tried to catch her breath, but the stays of her corset cut into her. She began sliding down the horse's side. The horse sidled. Visions of being trampled flew through her brain. She had to hang on. Scrambling to get her right leg on the other side of the horse made no difference. Groaning, she flung her right leg with all her might. She cleared the horse's back. And kept going. She clung harder to the mane, but her momentum swung her whole body to the right side of the horse.

The force of her body falling wrenched the mane from her grasp, and she was on her back in the cold mud, rain slapping her face. She threw her hands over her head to protect herself from the inevitable hooves she imagined she would feel any moment. What a terrible way to end, trampled in mud.

When nothing happened, she peered through her arms.

Josh's face crossed her vision. "Are you all right?" He sounded concerned, but she detected a hint of repressed laughter. His twinkling brown eyes and the dimples appearing in his cheeks confirmed her suspicions. He loved to pull pranks. Had he done this on purpose?

She clenched her jaw and stuck out a slimy glove. "Yes, I'm fine," she said tightly. The mud cushioned her fall. Nothing hurt but her pride. "Now help me up."

Josh hauled her to her feet. Letting go of his hand as quickly as possible, she tried to brush the mud off her dress before real-izing it was hopeless. Looking up at Josh, she saw the laughter tugging at his lips.

She glared at him. "Oh, go ahead and laugh. You probably threw me over that horse on purpose."

Laughter broke free of Josh, and he roared until it simmered to a chuckle.

Emily merely crossed her muddy arms waiting for him to finish. She would have tapped her toe if she could have freed it from the mud. "Shall we get on with it? I have better things to do than stand around all day in the rain. Like getting to Reedsville, for instance."

Josh rested his hands on his hips. "No point in being in a hurry about that. We won't get there any time soon."

She dropped her hands to her sides. "What do you mean by that? I thought that's where we were going."

"We *were* going there until the road washed out. Now we're going back to the way station."

She stomped her foot, a gesture made much less dramatic by the mud sucking at her shoe, resulting in a slow-motion squish. "*I'm* going to Reedsville even if I have to ride bareback all the way."

Josh snorted. "Yeah, we've seen how well you ride bareback." He trudged around the horse. "I'll get on first this time and pull you up." In one fluid motion, he bounded to the stagecoach boot and leaped for the horse's back, catching its mane and throwing his leg over in one sweep. Settled on its back, he leaned over and extended his hand, like he'd practiced that trick for the circus.

She crossed her arms again, staring at him. And the very large horse under him.

"What? Look, Emily, don't be ridiculous. We're both soaked to the skin, and I'd like to get warm sometime today. Give me your hand."

She continued to stare at him. "Only if we're going to Reedsville."

Josh blew out a sigh and pulled the brim down on his hat. "Out of the question."

She turned and began making her way to the stagecoach with great effort. She lifted up the oilskin flap over the boot and reached for her valise. She dragged it toward her and spun around, only to collide with Josh. The rain had veiled the sound of his steps.

She stared at Josh's chin mere inches away. Lifting her eyes to his, all she could think was that she'd never seen them such a deep shade of brown, like melted chocolate. She knew she was supposed to say something, but for the life of her she couldn't think of what it was.

She shivered, and his hands were on her in an instant, rubbing her arms.

"You're cold. We've got to get you dry before you take a chill. Maggie'd have my hide for sure if that happened."

Emily opened her mouth to speak, but Josh raised his hand from her arm to stop her. "No more arguing. I'll get you to Maggie's. It's closer than going back to the way station, but it's going to be tricky."

She looked away, absentmindedly reaching up to her neck, only to feel the whole back of her head coated with sticky goo. Pulling her hand away, she saw the mud coating her glove. With a sigh, she met his gaze. "I just want to get there."

He nodded, pursing his lips. "Can you climb up on the stage's boot?"

Setting her valise back on the boot, she boosted herself up until she was sitting on the edge and then swung her legs around.

"Good. You can mount from here."

Holding onto the flap, Emily stood, perching on the edge, while Josh remounted the horse.

While she was thrilled that the horse hadn't stomped her to

bits while she was on the ground, the thought of riding on the back of the huge beast made her gorge rise.

But it was the only way. And she'd done hard things before.

Taking his hand and gathering her skirts in the other, she let him pull her the short distance to the horse. Settling in front of Josh, her ankles were exposed. Although, really, how much more humiliated could she be after all that had happened today?

The horse shifted, and she bit back a yelp. Josh's arm tightened around her waist. Her panic ebbed a bit. He was an excellent horseman. He would keep her safe.

"My valise." She pointed back to the boot.

"Leave it. We'll come get it when we get the stage."

"I can't." She heard the panic in her voice but couldn't repress it. "I need it." She pointed to the horse where Josh had fashioned some blankets and ropes into a pack saddle of sorts to hold the mailbag. "You're bringing the mail. My valise is much smaller."

She felt rather than heard Josh take a deep breath and let it out before muttering something under his breath. He reached for the valise and hauled it up next to him.

"How come it's so heavy? What do you have in here, rocks?"

"No, just, uh, dresses and things. I have boots in there. Maybe that's why it's so heavy. They're pretty sturdy boots and they weigh quite a lot." She picked at the mud on her gloves. "You know, good leather isn't thin, so it's going to weigh more. And of course, women's skirts are fuller and use more material than men's clothes so certainly our bags will be heavier." She turned to see if her arguments had any effect on him.

He mumbled, "Hmm," and shook his head.

Josh spent some moments trying to figure out how to attach the valise to a horse without a saddle. Emily sat rigidly the whole time, hoping he wouldn't get frustrated and give up. She couldn't decide which panicked her more: the thought of staying on this horse until Reedsville or leaving her carpetbag behind.

Finally, he secured it around his own waist with extra-long

reins from the stage. Leading the other five horses, they headed to Reedsville.

And to Thomas.

Of all the ways she had imagined their reunion, appearing on horseback sopping wet and covered with mud had never entered her mind.

Chapter Three

I t was dark, with clouds covering the moon, when Josh and Emily rode into Reedsville. At least the rain had stopped. She was cold, tired, and dirty. Up until now, she had been hoping Thomas would be at Maggie's when she arrived. Now she desperately hoped he wouldn't be there to see her looking like a half-drowned rat that had crawled through the mud.

The front door to Maggie's boardinghouse opened the moment they rode by. Maggie had obviously been looking for them. The stage was hours overdue. "Oh my! Emily? Is that you?" She bustled out onto the porch. "What happened?"

"I'll explain later." Exhaustion thinned Josh's voice. "We'll come in through the kitchen." The horses hadn't even slowed. The barn was near, and they needed no encouragement.

They rounded the house and pulled up to the back porch steps. Maggie opened the back door, followed by James. Josh held Emily around the waist to lower her to the porch steps, but she was so stiff, she couldn't get her leg to move over the horse.

James stepped forward. "Here. Let me help."

Josh released his hold, and James put his hands around her waist and lifted her off the saddle. She moved her arms awkwardly to his shoulders, feeling more like she was flinging them. James set her on the porch, but when he let go of her, her legs buckled. He grabbed her upper arms.

Maggie hurried and put her arm around Emily, who towered over her. "Let's get you warm and dry."

She put her arm around Maggie's shoulders and let herself be led inside. She heard James offer to help Josh with the horses, and then the kitchen door closed behind them.

Maggie led her upstairs and into a guest room. Turning around, Emily was dismayed at the trail of mud she had left. "Oh, Maggie! Look what I've done to your floors."

"Don't worry yourself about it. It'll wash. Now you get out of those wet things while I bring up some warm water and dry clothes." Maggie left, closing the door behind her.

Where was she going to get dry clothes? The things in her valise were thoroughly soaked, and she certainly couldn't fit into any of Maggie's things. She sighed and removed her bedraggled hat that had looked so adorable this morning. She started to set it on the dresser, and then changed her mind and set it on the floor. At least Thomas wasn't here to see what a mess she was. She pulled off her gloves and tossed them next to the hat.

Seeing the buttonhook on the dresser, she started in on her shoes, bending over to unhook them because she didn't want to sit on the bed and get it muddy. She pulled off the first boot, hopping a bit and then leaning against the dresser for balance as she levered it off. Then the second boot. And her stockings. She was just starting on the buttons of her dress when there was a quick knock on the door.

She opened it, and Maggie came in, setting a pitcher and towels on the washbasin and then laying some clothes on the bed. "These are Sally's. They'll be a little short, but otherwise they should fit you. When you're ready, come downstairs and you can eat by the stove." And she was out the door.

Emily finished removing the rest of her wet, muddy clothes and hurried over to the washbasin. She poured water from the pitcher into the bowl and began to wash in the wonderfully warm water. Between combing and the remainder of the wash water, she was even able to get most of the mud off the back of her head.

Feeling mostly clean again, she slipped into Sally's clothes. Surprisingly, the dress was only a few inches too short. Sally must get her height from her father, as the only people shorter than Maggie were children.

When Emily came into the kitchen, Maggie had pulled up chairs next to the stove. Emily sat in one, and Maggie thrust a cup of tea in her hands. Emily took a sip. The liquid warmed its way down her throat and into her stomach. She was starting to thaw. A savory aroma—from the pot bubbling on the stove, she assumed—filled the kitchen. Her stomach contracted.

Maggie stirred the pot and then sat. "It's so good to see you back. Does this mean your grandfather recovered and you're back to teach?"

Emily put the cup to her lips and nodded before she took a sip. It was true, mostly.

"Did Josh know you were coming, or did you just show up at the station?"

The kitchen door opened as Maggie was speaking, and Josh answered. "She showed up at the station yesterday and talked me into this crazy adventure." He grinned and shook his head.

Emily smiled back at him. "It was a little colder and wetter than I thought it would be, but I had confidence in you, Josh. You got us back safely."

Maggie stood and poured Josh a cup of tea. He had dry clothes on, although his hair was still wet. He took the chair on the other side of the stove while Maggie began dishing up bowls of stew. She handed each of them one in exchange for their teacups.

Josh quickly blessed the food and began eating.

She couldn't remember when something had tasted so good.

Maggie hovered over them for a moment before asking Josh, "What happened to the stagecoach?"

He swallowed before answering. "There was a mudslide at the far side of the gorge. We got through with the horses, but we'll have to go back and dig out the stage. Preferably after it dries out a bit."

"Well I'm glad you two got home safe. That's all that matters."

Emily finished her stew. She was tired and wanted to go to bed, but she knew she would have a hard time sleeping unless she asked about Thomas. She had to make plans to see him. Trying to make her voice sound as unstrained as possible she asked, "How are Thomas and Seth doing? Is the logging company keeping them busy?" Her eyes darted from Josh to Maggie.

He shot Maggie a quick look.

Maggie's brow furrowed briefly before a dark veil settled over her features then softened.

Emily's stomach tightened, and her pulse increased. Learning to read people's expressions at a young age was a two-edged sword. It allowed her to pick out a person who would give her money for food to fill her empty belly. But sometimes she saw things she wished she hadn't. Like the bad news both Josh and Maggie were keeping from her. Had Thomas married someone else? Gone away? She wanted to scream but clasped her hands in her lap instead.

Maggie gave her a soft smile. "Well, Seth got married two months ago to Becca, Thomas's sister, who was at Willamette University when you came to teach."

"Well, that is good news. I'm looking forward to meeting her." But Emily knew that wasn't all the news. She waited, using all of her skills to keep her face neutral and her stomach from losing the stew she had just eaten.

Maggie glanced at Josh again. A shadow settled over his features. Sadness etched lines on his face.

She laid her hand on Emily's. "Thomas was killed last April in a logging accident."

Emily gave her a half-smile. She was so tired she was hearing things. She thought she heard Maggie say Thomas was killed. Why that was just silly! He couldn't be dead. She'd come all this way to tell him she was ready to marry him now. She even rode a horse bareback. She had ruined her shoes and hat just to see him.

The room spun, and then it went black.

JOSH DRAGGED his arm across his brow. He was working up a sweat despite the gray, drizzly day. Expelling a breath, he went back to mucking out the stalls while James took the mailbag to Fulton's Mercantile. James had come along nicely, learning about the stage business. While he didn't have a lot of experience driving the horses, he was still a big help.

And the mailbag survived Josh's improvisation. He couldn't leave it unattended, and with the road out, that mail contract was going to be his only source of income. It wouldn't be enough if the road didn't reopen soon. But it was better than nothing.

If he hadn't had Emily on his lap, he could have carried the mailbag. While it wasn't gentlemanly to even think it, he'd prefer her over the mailbag any day.

Once they were on their way to Reedsville, she hadn't complained. Occasionally, he'd feel a shiver course through her. She was cold; they both were. But she kept their minds off things by sharing about her visit to Seattle and reminiscing about some of their shared experiences in Portland and Reedsville. She was miserable, but she was helping them both keep their minds off their circumstances. She always had a wonderful way of putting people at ease.

Which made him doubly grateful he didn't have to be the one to tell her about Thomas. It was obviously a shock to her, but she was a strong woman. It wasn't like she'd been married to Thomas. She hadn't even seen him in nine months.

So what had been going on with her and Thomas?

He finished cleaning out the stalls and climbed into the hayloft. Tossing down hay, Josh heard the barn door squeak open for the second time this morning and reminded himself to oil the hinges.

"Anybody here?" Seth called out.

"Hey, Seth." Josh scrambled down from the hayloft as Seth rummaged around the work bench.

"Thought I'd come up and see if you needed a hand with the chores. With no farm animals and the logging camp shut down, I need to put my hand to something." Seth picked up the oil can. "Becca told me to come bother you."

Josh grinned as he slapped Seth on the stomach. "Married life's making you soft."

He returned a jab to Josh's shoulder. "I'm not complaining." He moved to the barn door and wiggled it back and forth causing it to squeak. "How bad is the road?"

"The whole gorge route is gone. Even with the horses alone, we had a hard time picking our way over all the debris. Only Providence kept us from any lame horses."

Seth squeezed oil onto the hinges while Josh moved the door to distribute the oil. "Getting the stage out doesn't sound like it's going to be easy."

"Nope. But we can't leave it out there for someone to take apart for firewood." He knew Seth felt bad enough about Josh putting up the Oregon Express to save Seth's logging company. He would do it again as sure as he'd take his next breath, but he couldn't afford to replace that stage. Not on top of everything else.

Seth stood and put the oil can back on the workbench. "We'll get some men and get that stage out of there, even if we have to take the whole mountain down." He paused a moment.

"Not that I'm questioning your judgment, but why did you risk it?"

Josh slid his eyes away. Seth knew about Pa, so it wasn't like he had anything to hide. But he didn't want to admit to dodging his own father. Plus, that wasn't the only reason. "It seemed like a good idea at the time. And I forgot to mention something."

"What's that?"

"I promised Emily Stanton I'd bring her here."

The information registered and understanding lit Seth's eyes. "She didn't know about Thomas, did she? Did you tell her?"

"I just couldn't bring myself to do it once I realized she didn't know. I don't know what to do with a crying woman. Maggie told her last night. Emily took it well. Before she fainted."

Seth raised his eyebrows. "Is she all right?"

Josh nodded and stepped out the barn door. "Let's go bother Maggie for a cup of coffee."

Seth followed. "Becca'll want to meet Emily."

Josh raised his eyebrows. When Becca had gone through Thomas's things after his death, she'd found a tintype of Emily and had asked Seth and Maggie about it. Becca clearly hadn't known about Emily. "What are you going to tell her?"

"What's to tell? I already told her Emily came here to teach. We don't really know any more than that, do we?"

"No, we don't." The men reached the kitchen door. Josh hesitated before opening it, his hand on the knob. "But why was Thomas the one with her photograph?"

AFTER BREAKFAST, Emily sat in Maggie's kitchen sipping coffee while Maggie did the dishes. She had refused Emily's offer of help. Lassitude as heavy as the clouds outside pressed heavily on her. The weight of trying to find peace in the midst of the bottom falling out of her plans and the loss of a dear friend. She twirled a pale blonde curl around her finger.

Oh, Lord, now what am I going to do? I thought I was supposed to come back here to marry Thomas. I thought that's what You wanted.

Turning down Thomas's proposal of marriage last spring was the right thing to do. She hadn't known his feelings for her were so strong. But during the months of caring for Silas, she wondered if Thomas's marriage proposal was God's way of giving her what she'd always wanted. After all, she cared for Thomas as a brother and a friend.

"You'll have to meet Becca while you're here." Maggie talked over her shoulder, up to her elbows in soapy dishwater. "I think the two of you will get along real well."

"I'd like to meet her."

Wet hands dripping over the dishpan, Maggie turned to face Emily. "I'm so sorry you didn't know about Thomas. It must have been a shock."

Emily swallowed. "It was. But there was no way for you to get in touch with me."

"Thomas didn't write you in Seattle?"

"No." She dropped her gaze to where her hands fidgeted on her lap. She felt Maggie's gaze on her. If Thomas hadn't told them about his proposal and her rejection, she wasn't going to. It didn't matter now, and she didn't want their pity. She'd had enough of that to last a lifetime.

She heard Maggie scrubbing a pan and ventured a look up.

Maggie continued talking. "You look like you need a good rest and some good food. The schoolteacher's cottage is empty. Sy and Cassandra O'Malley used it—oh, you probably didn't know that either. Cassandra Parsons married Sy O'Malley last March, and now they are both at Willamette University."

Emily smiled. "And her parents let her go? That is a miracle." She was happy for her friend, but now there was one less person in town she was close to.

Maggie flicked the water off her hands, hauled the dishpan to the back door, and tossed the water out. "Cassandra finally grew her own wings and flew the coop. The cottage hasn't been used in a few months. Stay here at the boardinghouse until we get it cleaned up and see what it needs." She hung the dishpan on its nail then looked at Emily. "Now I want you to spend the rest of the day in front of the fireplace. I won't have you getting sick under my roof."

She stood and gave Maggie a hug before heading to obey. With a book, she dutifully sat on the sofa in front of the fireplace. While she suffered no outward harm from yesterday's adventure, her soul agitated inside. The book provided a prop that suggested she was reading, but she would have been surprised if she'd turned a page. *Lord, what do I do now?*

She needed to approach Mr. Parsons. As head of the school board, he would be the one who would approve her teaching school again. And then there was the cottage Maggie mentioned. Lesson plans to be considered. At least now she would be able to teach longer since there was no question of her marrying.

But all of those seemed simple problems compared with the insurmountable one facing her right now. How was she going to return the money? Each day she waited was one more day someone could find it. How dare Silas put her in such a position! She would write and tell him exactly what she thought of what he'd done, but with the road washed out, the mail would be delayed. A telegram was out of the question. Too many people could see it.

The money! Where was her carpetbag?

Dropping the book, Emily stood. She had no idea what Josh had done with it. She was so cold and tired when she arrived, she wasn't thinking straight. But she couldn't believe she'd forgotten about the bag and just left it where anyone could get it. She had to find Josh and ask him where it was.

Thump! Thump! Thump!

The sound was coming from the back porch. She opened the kitchen door.

Maggie was knocking the dried mud off Emily's case with a broom.

Emily's heart leapt to her throat. If the carpetbag popped open… "No!"

Dropping the broom, Maggie spun around, green eyes wide. Her hand went to her heaving chest. "Goodness, you scared me half to death!"

Emily rushed forward and picked up the broom. "I'm sorry, Maggie. I didn't mean to. I just didn't want you to bother with the valise. I'll take care of it."

"I was just going to knock off what mud I could before bringing it inside and emptying it. Then we can give it a good scrubbing." She leaned closer to Emily. "I wouldn't open it out here where the men folk might see your underthings."

Scanning the yard between the boardinghouse and the barn, she saw Josh and Seth headed toward the house, deep in conversation.

Her pulse slowing, Emily gave Maggie a weak smile. "Oh, good. I was a little worried."

Maggie examined the carpetbag. "I think I got most of it off. If we wrap it in an old sheet, we could bring it in kitchen. Probably most of your clothes just need to dry out in front of the stove."

Panic welled in Emily's chest as her brain whirled frantically. How was she going to keep Maggie from opening her case? She ran her hand up the back of her neck. "How about you go find that sheet, and I'll try to get a little more mud off?"

"I'll be right back." Maggie disappeared through the door.

Emily watched her leave and then searched frantically for a hiding place without attracting the men's attention.

She ran out of time.

Josh and Seth mounted the steps. "Emily Stanton. It's good

to see you again." Seth doffed his hat. "I gather your adventures with Josh have left you no worse for wear?"

She forced her lips to turn up and gave a slight nod. "It was. . . an adventure. Not one I'd care to repeat anytime soon, however. But Josh is very good at what he does, as clearly I am here safe and sound." Her gaze met Josh's, and warmth spread through her chest.

His eyes crinkled a bit at the corners, and his shoulders straightened a touch.

Well, he should be proud of his accomplishment. There was no one she would trust more with her life. Which was what their adventure had felt like, though he had handled it with aplomb like it was a part of his routine. Surely that's why she felt so connected to him and had this unreasonable desire to tell him about the money and ask for his help.

She swung the back door open. "Maggie has just put on a fresh pot of coffee, and I believe there are some cookies left in the jar if James hasn't finished them off." She smiled broadly. *Hurry inside, please. I'm running out of time.*

They levered off their boots and stepped in the house. Could they move any slower? Maggie would be back any minute. She shut the door behind them and heard Maggie's voice in the kitchen. That should buy her a bit more time as Maggie served the men.

She searched her surroundings again. The flower beds? Under the porch? Anything would do for now, and she could move it later. She snapped open the valise and drew out the leather pouch, hiding it in the folds of her skirts as she scurried down the porch steps, the drizzle quickly dampening her hair.

The flowers weren't tall enough to cover the bag, and there wasn't a big enough hole under the porch. She chewed her lip and swiveled her head around the yard. She was running out of time. The barn! There'd have to be someplace to hide it there.

Emily skittered across the yard and yanked on the barn door. It slid open smoothly, and she slipped inside. The smell of freshly cut lumber, hay, animals, and leather filled her nose. A scraping noise came from the back of the barn. As her eyes adjusted to the light, she found the spot. A box in a corner held a pile of old tools and equipment. Before whoever else was in here could spot her, she moved some of the tools around and stuffed the bag deep in the box. Standing back, she made sure it wasn't visible. She hurried outside and had just reached the porch stairs when Maggie came out the door.

She raised her eyebrows. "Did you get any more mud off?"

"Uh, I think so. I thought"—she gestured back towards the barn—"that straw might help get some more off, but it was too flimsy." The tension in her shoulders eased. That was one benefit of her past. She could think on her feet and quickly come up with a plausible lie.

"Well, let's wrap it up and get it inside. You got wet again, and I'm afraid you'll catch your death of a cold."

Helping Maggie unfold the sheet, Emily slowly released her pent-up breath and railed at Silas one more time in her thoughts.

Chapter Four

McKay's legs cramped from being folded in one position too long, but a flash of color at the back door told him his patience had been rewarded. The things he did for Dillon. If ever there was any truth to the good-twin, bad-twin adage, he and Dillon were living proof of it. His whole life had been getting Dillon out of one scrape or another. Though this time it was much more than a scrape. And this had better be the end of it.

Voices floated over to his position in the damp woods as five people left the boardinghouse and climbed into a wagon. It had taken three days, but finally it looked like no one would be home. His pulse quickened now that his goal was so near, but he forced himself to wait. The wagon left the boardinghouse, and still he waited until the only sounds he heard were a few birds and his own breathing.

Straightening his legs, his knees almost buckled, but he flexed them a few times until he was sure they'd hold his weight. He scanned the area before leaving the covering of the woods. Satisfied, he crossed the meadow and walked to the boarding-house and climbed the back porch steps.

EMILY COULDN'T CONCENTRATE on the passage Seth read in the combination church and schoolhouse. It wasn't their week for the circuit preacher, but the town still met for a time of singing and fellowship, with the men taking turns reading Scripture.

Josh sat next to her. She carefully kept her skirts away from his leg, but even though they weren't touching, his presence was palpable. Was he treating her differently? Had he found the money in the barn? Surely he would have said something if he had. And then what would she say? The thought of lying to him made her want to squirm. She pushed it out of her head and tried to focus on the passage Seth was reading from.

But she couldn't. No, if anyone had found the pouch of bank notes, she would have heard. Wouldn't she? Maggie hadn't let her out of sight all day yesterday since it was raining and she was afraid Emily would catch cold. So Emily hadn't had a chance to see if there was a better hiding place in the barn. Instead, she had worked up lesson plans, and what she would say to Mr. Parsons today at church.

And composed the one hundredth letter to Silas in her mind. She couldn't decide on which tone to take. Angry, insulted, grateful, understanding, conciliatory. Undecided, she still hadn't put pen to paper.

She supressed a sigh when Sally nudged her. Everyone else was standing to sing. Out of the corner of her eye, Emily saw Josh study her while she mouthed the words, singing only out of habit, her mind on what she needed to happen after the service.

With the final prayer and benediction said, she made her way outside and away from Josh, giving a few perfunctory hellos and nods while scanning the crowd for Mr. Parsons. Her height gave her the advantage.

She spotted Mrs. Parsons first, her fashionable flowerpot hat —much like Emily's recently ruined one—marking her as more well-to-do than most of the women wearing simple poke bonnets. She scurried over before anyone else could engage them.

"Mr. and Mrs. Parsons, how do you do on this lovely Lord's day? Isn't the sunshine delightful after all that rain?" Emily put effort into giving her most becoming smile.

"Miss Stanton, I heard you had returned but I could hardly believe it. We assumed you'd run off for good." Mr. Parsons scratched his bald spot before putting his hat on.

Emily opened her mouth, her excuse ready, when Mrs. Parsons laid a hand on her arm. "It actually was a providence that you were gone so long. Our Cassandra held the position of schoolmarm and did a wonderful job. The children enjoyed her very much. And now she and her husband, Sy, are pursuing higher education in Salem at Willamette University. They both are quite accomplished."

"I had heard that and was so pleased for her. I was only sorry that I couldn't give her my best wishes in person. But that is precisely—"

"We must hurry home. My wife has left a delicious roast in the oven, and it would be a shame for it to burn." Mr. Parsons pulled his wife's hand through his arm.

"If I could have just a—"

"Good to see you again, Miss Stanton." Mrs. Parsons tugged on her husband's arm, and they began to move away.

Emily took two quick steps and blocked their way, stopping them. "I won't take but a minute. I wouldn't want your roast to burn, either. However, I did want to discuss the teaching position. I am ready to begin—"

Mr. Parsons nudged his wife to the side, around Emily. "This isn't the time or place to discuss business. If you have something to say, you can find me at the hotel during the week. Good day."

Emily stared after them. That wasn't how she had predicted it would go. Looking around, she realized no one had noticed what had happened. Thank goodness for small favors. Folks were visiting in groups around the churchyard.

Needing a moment to compose herself before facing anyone, she walked around to the far side of the building. Leaning against it, she took a deep breath. She had to get the school-teaching job. If any more of her plans fell apart, she didn't know what she would do. Besides, who else could teach? They needed her.

She pushed away from the wall and massaged her temples. Maggie would want to know what was going on. Maybe she could plead a headache. But then Maggie would think she was getting sick and would confine her to the house again. This was becoming a tangled knot. One she might not be able to undo.

She rounded the corner to join the others and caught herself just in time to avoid colliding with Becca. Dressed in a lovely pink dress with jet buttons, Becca was more stylish than anyone else in Reedsville, even Mrs. Parsons. Emily glanced down at the well-worn day dress that had been stylish a few years ago. Once again, she felt like a little girl wearing someone else's cast offs.

"You must be Emily." The petite blonde gave Emily's arm a squeeze. "I'm Becca."

Emily smiled. "Yes. It's so good to meet you. Thomas's infamous little sister." She wished she could pull the words back in. Why hadn't she thought more carefully? Surely Becca didn't want to be reminded of her brother.

Becca giggled. "Don't believe all the stories he told about me. I was the innocent one. He always got me into trouble." Her smile faded. "I'm sorry you didn't know about his—" Her voice caught. "Well, what happened before you got here. That must have been a difficult way to find out."

Emily swallowed and nodded. She didn't want to talk about it. Her mind searched wildly for a way to change the subject without being rude.

Becca's green eyes held hers for a moment. "I told Maggie

you all are invited for Sunday dinner at my house. That's why I came looking for you."

"Oh?" There went her chance to plead a headache. How was she supposed to be polite for an entire afternoon? "Well, I—"

"There you two are." Maggie bustled over to them. "I see you've met. Becca, I've got a pie just begging to be eaten. I thought I'd send one of the men over to get it, if that would work with you."

"That would be wonderful. But why don't Emily and I get it? I like to take advantage of the sunny days when I can." She stepped forward and linked her arm through Emily's. "Besides, we can get better acquainted."

Emily pasted on a smile and nodded.

MCKAY YANKED open the back door of the boardinghouse and slipped in. He scanned the kitchen before moving through the dining room and parlor. Then he headed upstairs, his footsteps loud in the empty house. He opened drawers and examined clothes until he found the room he thought was hers. Yes, he recognized the dress on the peg as the one she was wearing on the ferry. He glanced out the window and was pleased to see it looked directly out to the woods. He could keep an eye on her room from there if need be. But he hoped he didn't need to.

He opened the dresser and pulled everything out, filtering the items through his hands. Then he yanked the drawers all the way out and looked inside the dresser casing. Pulling it away from the wall, he looked behind it. Impatient, he looked under the bed. It had to be here somewhere!

He jerked the quilts and muslin sheets from the mattress. He ran his hands all along the mattress and resorted to pulling out half the ticking to assure himself nothing was hidden inside.

Where was it? Anger surged within him. Why did Dillon always put him in these situations? He yanked her dresses off the pegs and threw them across the room. He picked up the wash basin and jerked it over his head.

His reflection in the mirror stopped him. In that moment, he looked just like Dillon. He glanced around the room, lowered the basin, and set it down. What was he doing? What had Dillon gotten him into? He had only planned to come in, find her bag, and take back the money. He hoped she hadn't even seen it, but he figured that was a pretty slim chance at this point. Tearing up her room like this was only going to alert people something was wrong.

He shook his head in disgust. He would never normally act like this. It was only because he was trying to get Dillon out of another mess. This would be the last one. He'd make sure of it. One way or another.

He stuffed clothes back into drawers and shoved the drawers back into the dresser. He pushed the straw back into the mattress ticking and tossed the linens back on the bed, haphazardly straightening them out. Dresses went back on the pegs while he decided what to do next.

The bag was missing. Where would she have put the bag? If he could find it, maybe he could find the money. If he could return it, things would go easier on Dillon.

Voices floated up to him from the street. They were getting closer to the house. He dashed into what appeared to be the mother's room, which had a window on the front of house. Two women were walking up the street.

One was her.

He had to get that money, the sooner the better. And that woman was the key.

EMILY HAD to admit the warm sunshine on her back and the fresh air had done much to alleviate her headache. Becca was friendly and easy to talk to; Emily felt like they were old friends.

Maybe if she had a true friend—other than Pastor Luke's wife—
she could tell the whole story. A verse from Ecclesiastes floated
through her mind about two being better than one. It would be
a relief to share the burden with someone else.

But images of people accusing her, faces full of anger and
disappointment, kept her mouth shut. Of all those people, only
Mrs. Luke had stood by her. Everyone else had deserted her.
That would happen this time too. No, she couldn't share this
burden and face rejection again. She had determined to become
a respectable member of society in Reedsville. And that couldn't
happen if townspeople found out about her past.

"Emily?"

She came out of her reverie to notice they had stopped in
front of Maggie's.

Becca raised her eyebrows.

"I'm sorry, what did you say?"

Becca laughed. "I daydream too. Especially on beautiful days
like today. Let's go get that pie of Maggie's. This walk has worked
up my appetite."

They hurried around to the back porch steps. Becca grabbed
the back door which stood wide open. "Oh, Maggie'd be so mad
if she saw this. Someone must have left the back door open. I
bet there's a thousand flies inside." They stepped into the
kitchen.

"So, do you have my old room?" Becca looked around the
kitchen.

"The one at the top of the stairs?" At Becca's nod, Emily
answered, "Yes."

"Be sure to look out the window early one morning. Especially after it's just rained. It's a sight to behold." Becca spotted
what she was looking for. "Emily, you're tall. Could you get that
basket up there for me? Josh probably put it away—or James—
because I know Maggie can't reach that high."

Emily stretched on her tiptoes to get the basket. Doing so
caused her shoes to pinch. Her pointy-toed shoes were lovely,

and she was grateful she was able to remove all the mud from them. But they weren't practical. She hadn't planned on walking back from church in them. She handed the basket to Becca.

"I'm going to change into my boots. These shoes are hurting my feet."

"Go ahead. I'm going to wrap up this pie."

Up in her room, Emily grabbed the buttonhook off the dresser. One of her chemises was hanging out of the drawer, so she tucked it back in before sitting on her bed. Unhooking the buttons on her shoes, she noticed the bed felt a little lumpy. She pulled off her shoes, stood and looked at the bed.

"I really must not have been paying attention this morning to not make my bed." Lining her shoes up against the wall, she looked for her boots.

"What's going on? Is someone playing a trick?" She looked more carefully at the bed then around the room. Nothing was exactly where it should be. Was this Josh's welcome home surprise? He liked to play pranks, but she didn't think he'd go through her clothes. Besides, he drove them this morning to church. He didn't have time to come up here without her knowing.

A chill washed over her, and her stomach flipped upside down. She sank on the bed.

"Emily?"

She let out a gasp and was on her feet before she saw it was Becca.

"When you didn't come downstairs, I came to make sure you're feeling well." Becca's voice was soft, but Emily saw her eyes scan the room.

Her brain whirled trying to come up with an excuse. If she admitted she left her room like this, Becca would think she was terribly sloppy. Emily prided herself on being neat and orderly. But if she admitted she didn't know how her room got like this, Becca would start asking questions and likely ask the men to come investigate. Emily sighed and put her hand to her head.

"You have a headache, don't you?" Becca took her hand and tugged her to sit on the bed, then sat next to her. "I suppose it's quite a lot to take in all at once. I remember when I first came back, I felt off balance for days. Everything had changed, and yet, for some reason, I had expected everything to be just as it was when I had left." She patted Emily's hand. "Would—"

A floorboard squeaked. Emily's heart pounded.

Becca looked around. "I wonder if someone came to see why we were taking so long." She stood. "Although it sounded like it came from upstairs." She walked toward the door. "I wonder if Josh…" Leaning out the doorway into the hall she called, "Hello? We're upstairs." She paused a minute and then turned back to the room.

Emily swallowed. "It was probably just the house creaking, drying out from the rain." She hoped her voice sounded normal to Becca, not tight and pinched like it sounded to her ears.

"I'm sure you're right. Would you rather stay here and rest—"

"Oh, no. I'm fine." Emily jumped up. "Let's go before they do send out a search party." She forced a smile.

Becca gave her a genuine one in return.

McKay waited for the women to leave and then waited some more. He cautiously stepped forward and peeked into the hall. He listened. Hearing nothing, he hurried downstairs. He went into the kitchen and glanced in the pantry. Down the basement stairs, he scanned the small root cellar. Nothing.

It had to be somewhere!

He hurried through the rest of the house, looking out the windows frequently to see if anyone else was coming. He couldn't find it. Could Dillon have been wrong? No, he had pointed her out, and McKay himself had seen her board the stagecoach. It was her. The money had to be here somewhere.

But he'd been here too long as it was. He'd have to come back later. He peered out the kitchen window and then exited through the kitchen door.

He headed across the yard to the barn. There were a million places to hide things in a barn. He would probably have to make a second trip to search the place. Easing the barn door open, he slipped inside and let his eyes adjust to the dimness.

And there it was.

The bag his twin brother had stuffed the money into on the ferry hung from a peg on the wall. With a sinking feeling, he snatched it down.

It was empty.

Chapter Five

Piled in the wagon, the group rode back from Becca and Seth's house in the fading light. Emily sat between Josh and Maggie, enjoying a moment of contentment. It had been a good afternoon. Emily's headache had gone away shortly after dinner, but Becca made sure Emily didn't do anything that might cause it to return.

Becca was several years younger, but a bubble of cautious hope arose in Emily's chest. She liked Becca and envied her a bit too. Unlike the girls in her past, Becca seemed genuinely interested in Emily. It was a strange, but good, feeling.

A steady ache joined the bubble thinking about how happy Seth and Becca were. He couldn't keep his eyes off Becca, and she glowed when she talked about him or looked in his direction.

Emily knew she and Thomas would have had companionship and respect, but not a romantic kind of love, even though that thought seemed somehow traitorous. Not all, maybe not even most, were destined to marry for love. She missed him, certainly, but as a friend. His death hadn't left a hole in the fabric of her life, just a sore spot in her heart. Still, she longed for the sense of security and belonging he had offered.

She was still considered an outsider, but maybe over time, she could become a part of the community and gain respectability. Yes, being the schoolmarm would provide that.

As long as she could get the money back to Silas before anyone discovered it. And no one could ever know, or she'd be thrown out on her ear. And the idea of starting over somewhere else yet again… Well, she couldn't even entertain it.

Back at the boardinghouse, Maggie was muttering as she shut the doors to the basement and the pantry.

Emily was about to head upstairs when Maggie called her.

"Emily, did—"

Sally came running downstairs, interrupting. "Mama, have you seen my room?"

"Not since I woke you up this morning. Why?"

"I think James is playing a trick on me. Everything's a little bit mussed. Come see."

Emily stilled. Her earlier fear flooded back. Was it possible someone had been in Sally's room too? Maybe it didn't have anything to do with the money. But this had never happened before. Nothing ever happened in Reedsville. Maggie's doors didn't even have locks. Would anyone think it was a coincidence that it happened after Emily arrived?

Maggie frowned. "It's not like James to go into your room. Could he have been looking for something?"

"I don't know what. It doesn't look like anything's missing."

The three headed up to Sally's room. Maggie looked around from the doorway and then stepped into her own room. Emily saw Sally's bed had been treated much like her own.

Maggie came back. "My room looks the same. Someone's been in here. I wondered why the pantry and basement doors were open. After finding mice in the basement, I always keep that door closed. Sally, go ask your brother and Josh to come in here."

Sally hurried down the stairs. Maggie turned to Emily. "Your room too?"

She nodded. It had happened to everyone. Her knees weakened, and she sat on her bed. Nothing pointed specifically to Emily.

Maggie put her hands on her ample hips. "Did you notice anything when you and Becca came to get the pie?"

Emily started to shake her head no. How could she explain not telling them what she saw earlier? Then she remembered Becca had seen her room. "I came upstairs to change into my boots and noticed one of my chemises was outside the drawer. And when I sat on my bed it was lumpy, like it hadn't been made well. I just thought I was tired this morning and hadn't been paying attention."

Nothing else had been touched, though, when she and Becca had been here. The rest of the house had been fine.

Blood rushed to her head. The open door when she and Becca had come in. The floorboard squeak. He was here. He was still in the house when she and Becca had come home.

A shiver tracked through her body. Sunday dinner sat heavy on her stomach.

Maggie headed down the hall, peering into each of the guest rooms.

Should Emily tell her? Would it matter? He hadn't hurt Becca or her. They'd probably just surprised him. Whoever he was. But she knew. It was somehow related to the money.

The kitchen door banged open followed by voices and footsteps. "Let's go downstairs." Maggie came out of the last guest room. "We'll tell Josh and James about it and go from there."

Emily followed Maggie downstairs and into the parlor, which had suffered the same fate as the rest of the house. The desk had papers sticking out. Books sat askew on the bookshelf. Cushions and pillows weren't in their places. Josh, James, and Sally joined them. Maggie told them what they had discovered upstairs.

Josh listened. "Mind if I take a look?"

"Not at all," Maggie replied. "James, go fetch the sheriff." James nodded and was out the door.

Emily was surprised. "Reedsville has a sheriff?" Yet more change while she was gone.

"Yep," Josh said. "Michael Riley. After all the trouble we had last spring and summer, the county sheriff told us we needed our own. Riley got elected sheriff the same time Parsons became mayor."

"Mr. Parsons is the mayor?" Things certainly had changed while she was gone. Maybe whomever was in the house was related to the changes in the town, not to the money. It was a hopeful thought, but not likely.

Josh laughed. "Oh, yeah. You missed one interesting campaign. He ran against Bill Benchly."

"The saloon owner?" Her jaw dropped. Her eyebrows must have been near her hairline. What had happened to the little town at the end of the Oregon Trail?

Josh laughed. "See what happens when you go away for a while?" He squeezed her shoulder on his way upstairs. The heat from his hand bled through her bodice.

To cover her discomfort, she started to move a pillow aside so she could sit on the sofa and then stopped. "I suppose we should leave everything as it is until the sheriff gets here."

"I'm sure you're right," Maggie said. "Let's go sit in the kitchen. If I have to look at this mess without being able to straighten it, I'll go crazy."

Emily, Sally, and Maggie moved into the kitchen and sat at the table. Emily clasped her hands in her lap. She could hear Josh moving around upstairs.

"I can't think who would have done this." Maggie shook her head. "It's not the time of year we have strangers in town. No boarders or drifters looking for work at the logging camps or the mines."

Emily looked at her hands in her lap. Her knuckles were white. She loosened her grip, noticing red marks from her own fingers on her hands. She was the only new person in town. She hadn't done it, but nobody would believe her. Nobody ever believed her. Especially when she was telling the truth. She had to get in touch with Silas and get the money back to its rightful owner before something worse happened.

The front door opened, and Maggie went to greet the sheriff. She heard Josh come downstairs and the two of them explain what they discovered. As they talked, Emily tried to picture Michael Riley. She barely remembered him from church. Mostly she knew the parents of her students. He was single, she thought, so she wouldn't have interacted with him much. But the faint impression she had of him was a quiet, steady man.

She heard footsteps approach the kitchen and looked up. There stood Michael Riley, with Josh behind him. She swallowed and reached her hand up to the nape of her neck, patting her hair in place.

His dark hair had a touch of silver at the temples. He was a bit shorter than Josh and stockier. His eyes were very dark. She didn't remember ever noticing his eyes before.

"Miss Stanton, it's good to see you. I'm sure quite a few parents are glad to have you back, although I'm not sure all their children are." He gave her a kind smile.

She pasted on a smile. "Thank you. It's good to be back."

"Maggie and Josh have told me what they saw. Did you see anything?"

She took even breaths then related what she had already told Maggie.

"How did the rest of the house look?"

"We only came into the kitchen. I didn't notice anything unusual, but I wasn't paying attention."

"Is anything of yours missing? Any valuables?"

She twisted a curl around her finger. "No. I don't have any."

"Okay. Thanks. Maggie, want to show me upstairs?"

Maggie led the sheriff upstairs, but Josh pulled out a kitchen chair and sat. "You okay?"

Emily nodded. "Yes. Nothing's missing is it?"

"Doesn't look like it." He gave her a long look.

Instead of feeling scrutinized, she felt… protected.

"You look like something's bothering you. You're safe here. My cabin's just out back, and James is here. We'll get some locks put on the doors in the morning. You don't have anything to worry about."

"Thank you. I'll be fine. I'm still tired from the trip. A day or two and I should be fine." She smiled at him, wanting to keep the warmth in his eyes wrapped around her. "Thanks for your concern."

He nodded then squeezed her hand.

Tingles traveled from her hand throughout her body. She truly wasn't herself.

Maggie and the sheriff came downstairs. "It's probably just a drifter looking for money or valuables, taking advantage of the fact that you all were at church. I'll talk to Parsons to see if there's anyone new staying at his hotel. But I suspect whoever was here is long gone by now." The sheriff put on his hat. "I'll let you know if I find out anything."

"Thank you, Michael," Maggie said. "Are you sure I can't talk you into staying for supper?"

"It's mighty tempting, but no, ma'am. Thank you, though. I'll see myself out."

Josh stood to follow him out, and Maggie started for the parlor, no doubt not able to wait one minute before straightening things.

Emily drummed her fingers on the table. Josh hadn't mentioned the barn so she supposed it meant the intruder hadn't been there. She was dying to go see for herself but couldn't think of one good excuse to go to the barn. But first thing in the morning she'd be out there. She had to find someplace more secure for the money.

And then she had to find some way to contact Silas. Washed out road or not.

MAKING sure the fire had caught, Josh lowered himself into his favorite chair in his cabin behind the barn and pulled his boots off. It had been a long, tiring day. No one had ever had their home broken into in Reedsville, and he couldn't figure out why it had happened to Maggie now. It was probably as Riley had supposed. A drifter looking for money.

The only trouble they'd had was last summer when those drifters attacked Becca. But then they really hadn't been drifters. McCormick had hired them to scare her off. Now that he was no longer a problem, they shouldn't have anything to worry about. But that didn't reassure the unease in his gut.

His cabin was close to the boardinghouse, but not close enough if there was real trouble. Sure, James was there. And Maggie was formidable herself. Even with the strangers they had in the boardinghouse, there had never been a time Josh had felt they were in danger. And he didn't think that now… exactly.

Emily's face swam in his mind. She was no shrinking violet. Though she never said much about her past, Josh knew enough to know her growing up years weren't easy. But she was determined. When he first met her, she was working at Mrs. Hanson's hotel studying to pass her teacher's exam. And she did.

He had enjoyed sitting next to her at church, more than he thought. His attention was on her more than on the passage Seth had read, he'd have to confess. He couldn't help but notice something was preoccupying her as well. Why he was compelled to help her, he didn't know. Sure, it was a shame what had happened Thomas, and though no one said it outright, clearly she and Thomas had some sort of understanding. It was just natural sympathy, that was it.

Setting his boots on the floor, he looked up at the letter sitting on the mantle, where it had sat for the past several days. Reluctantly, he pushed himself out of his chair, grabbed the letter, and sat back down. Firelight flickered on the flimsy paper, casting deep shadows behind it. Shoulders tensing, he perused the words, then tapped it on his knee. He didn't want to open it. The day had been tiring enough. He didn't want to add anything to it, he just wanted to go to bed.

Being from Pa, Josh had a pretty good guess as to what it contained. He almost tossed it in the fire, unopened, as the familiar memories raced through his brain: Ma taking in wash to provide for the family while Pa drank their money away. Pa drunk or sleeping off a drinking binge. Ma in bed, weak and pale, with a faded quilt pulled up to her chin. Her funeral.

He stared at the fire, trying to blot out the pictures. He'd been putting it off, and he knew it was past time to open it. Breaking the seal, he scanned the letter quickly and frowned. Anger gave way to disbelief as he read again more slowly, and then one more time to see if the words had changed. Josh dropped his hand over the side of the chair and let the letter slide to the floor. He rubbed his face.

Forgiveness. Pa had asked for forgiveness.

Josh didn't want to give it to him. Part of him wanted Pa to pay for what he had done, for how he had hurt the family. But only God could hold Pa accountable for his actions.

What difference would his forgiveness make? Did it make Pa feel better? He'd repented before and sworn he'd never do it again. And then he did.

A verse from Matthew floated through Josh's mind. "I say not unto thee, until seven times; but, until seventy times seven."

He knew what the Bible said. And he would forgive him. Again. But did he have to open his heart to the deceit and the lies every time? Unforgiveness wasn't a burden he wanted to carry. But he didn't want to trust Pa either.

Bracing his hands on his thighs, he pushed out of the chair and shoved the whole issue from his mind and went to bed.

Chapter Six

The weather looked like it was going to hold so the men left early the next morning to examine the washed-out road and see if it could be repaired. Emily was a little nervous now that Josh wouldn't be able to install the locks as he had promised, but she was grateful the men would be out of the barn.

She hurried through her morning routine and slipped out when Maggie wouldn't notice her missing, careful to let the door close softly.

Hoping Maggie didn't happen to be looking out a back window, Emily hurried across the yard to the barn and slipped inside. The musty hay tickled her nose.

Her carpetbag was missing. She had left it to dry on a peg on the wall. She spun, searching the barn. Had Maggie taken it inside? Or one of the men? She'd have to ask. It would give her a good excuse for being out here.

But what if Maggie hadn't moved it? Had the person who had ransacked boardinghouse taken it? Why? It didn't have much value of itself. It didn't appear he took anything, so he wouldn't need it to carry items away.

Unless he knew the money had been in the valise at one point.

She closed her eyes. She had just about convinced herself that Michael Riley was right. That it was a drifter looking for valuables. That it had nothing to do with the money. Now she knew better.

She moved over to the tool bin, scanning the area for any sign that someone had been looking around her hiding spot. Many of the tools were missing. She suspected the men had taken the shovels and picks with them to the washed-out road.

She pushed the remaining tools around and found the pouch where she had left it. Her hands shook in relief. And yet a twinge of disappointment settled through her. If someone had found it, then it wouldn't be her problem anymore.

She rubbed the back of her neck. Would there be a way to let the person who was looking for the money find it? Without someone else finding it first? Maybe it was their money anyway.

If that were the case, why didn't they just come up to her and ask her for it? Unless they thought she stole it. Then why not go to the sheriff? She groaned. There were too many knots to work out of this problem, too much information she didn't know. She'd stick with her original plan until she knew more.

Clutching the pouch, she scanned the barn for a better hiding place. She'd been in here too long as it was. If Maggie came looking for her, she wouldn't have a good excuse. Other than the tool bin, there was nowhere to hide the money at the front of the barn. The tack room was used too frequently.

Her gaze wandered. She tried to think of all the places Silas had hidden money when she was growing up. Straw and dirt scattered across the floor. Maybe there was a loose floorboard. The barn had been newly rebuilt after last year's fire so she didn't have much hope. But she was running out of options.

She pulled a hoe out of the tool bin and used the handle to tap across the floor. Thump. Thump. Thump. Thud. Emily stopped and tapped again. Not exactly hollow sounding but different. Maybe a gap big enough to squeeze the bag in? She knelt down and brushed away dirt and straw. Running her hands along the joints, she tugged, looking for a loose spot.

A knot hole. That would work. She stuck her finger in the hole and yanked up. The board pulled free, and she lost her balance, landing on her backside. Relief weakened her muscles as she righted herself and peered in the hole.

Shiny black metal with a dial and a handle filled the hole. A safe.

She sat stunned for a moment and then smiled. Josh obviously thought of the same hiding places she did. She returned the board to its place and smeared dirt and straw back over it until she was satisfied it didn't look disturbed.

A safe would be a good place to hide the money until it could be returned. But she couldn't imagine explaining the situation to Josh. If he knew she'd been a thief, and that Silas still was, it would only be natural for him to think she had something to do with stealing this money. What did he really know about her anyway? That she had worked at a hotel in Portland, gone to the same church as he did, and taught school. None of that precluded her being a thief.

Besides, the last time she'd been completely honest with people, she'd hurt the only people she loved and had nearly gone to jail. She never wanted to go through that again. And it would be worse to risk Josh's rejection, someone she greatly respected. She didn't want to see the look of disgust in his eyes. No, she'd do this the way she'd planned.

She was running out of time. She couldn't shake the feeling creeping up her neck that someone was watching her. Any moment the barn door would open, and she'd be caught trying to explain. She hurried toward the back of the barn.

The horse stalls. She stopped, her stomach tensing. There was no place else. She took a deep breath and started down the aisle. The horses seemed huge and loomed over the stall doors.

One nickered near her ear and she jumped. She hunkered

down, her heart pounding. *I can't do this.* Tears welled up, and she squeezed her eyes closed. *Not now. Pull yourself together. You've been through worse.*

She opened her eyes, took a deep breath, and forced herself to straighten. Standing still, she looked around, purposely making her muscles relax. One horse looked back at her but didn't move. None of the rest seemed interested in her.

The two stalls at the end were empty where Josh and James had taken the horses they were riding today. Josh kept his stalls clean. She knew she couldn't just hide it in the straw or he'd find it. But maybe…

She entered the next-to-last stall and crouched down. Under the manger, she could pull open a space between it and the barn wall. Wiggling it to loosen it, she could just squeeze the pouch behind it. With a final shove, she wedged it in tightly. There! She sat back on her haunches and wiped her arm across her forehead. Glancing up, she started. The horse in the next stall had put his head over the wall, eyeing her.

"Hey there, boy. How are you doing?" Her voice shook, but she didn't know if horses noticed those kinds of things. Could they smell fear? She eased back toward the door, so she could stand up without coming face to face with him. Or her.

A whoosh split the silence as the barn door opened. Emily's heart thrummed again. Should she hide until the person left, or just come out like nothing was going on? People almost always took things at face value, Silas had told her. She stepped out into the aisle.

Sally stood by the door, her face in shadow as she was backlit by the sun streaming in through the doorway.

Emily walked quickly between the stalls, not wanting to say anything in case talking spooked the horses.

"Emily?"

She took two final steps and cleared the last stall. "Yes, it's me Sally."

"I didn't know you were out here. Mama sent me to see if there were any rags. She's in one of her cleaning moods."

"I didn't see any. Maybe in the tack room?"

Sally stepped over there and looked in. "Yes. Here they are." She disappeared for a moment and reappeared with her hands full of rags.

"Would your mother or Josh have moved my valise from out here? Is there somewhere in particular that you put things like that? I can't find mine. It was hanging on that peg."

Sally thought for a moment. "I don't know. I—"

The sun disappeared, throwing the barn into darkness. Emily and Sally both hurried out the door. A cloud had passed in front of the sun and more were piling up in the sky. So much for the weather holding. "Let's get inside. The men will be soaked by the time they get here."

She tugged the barn door shut and followed Sally into the house.

THE FRIENDLY BANTER BETWEEN JOSH, Seth, and James fell off as they got closer to the mudslide area. This part of the road didn't look too bad, certainly not as bad as where he and Emily got stuck. He almost laughed out loud at his image of her that day: dripping wet, muddy, and still determined to get her way.

How was she doing? The way she kept twirling her hair around her finger and clasping her hands last night proved she was more afraid than she would admit. Unfortunately, he wouldn't be able to get those locks installed today like he promised. It wasn't raining right now, and they needed to take advantage of that to check out the road. But first thing tomorrow he'd get them put in. Maybe that would make her feel more secure.

He'd never thought about her much when she lived here

before, but now there was something different about her. He couldn't put his finger on it, but his mind puzzled over it.

They rounded the bend, and Josh reined in. He pulled his mind back to the present and scanned the area. The stage sat in mud up to its hubs. The road was unrecognizable. It was as bad as he remembered. He had hoped the concern of getting Emily and the horses home had made the situation seem worse than it actually was. Nope, it was just as bad.

He rubbed his hand over his face then dismounted, promptly sinking into the mud.

He untied the shovel from the back of his saddle and joined Seth, who was already off his horse and slogging his way toward the stage. They began by attacking the mud in front of the wheels. Josh hoped they could create a firm path for the stage to travel on. The mud was wet and heavy. This was going to be more work and take longer than he originally thought. He tried to throw big shovelfuls of mud away from the road, but soon his shoulders and back protested, and he had to be content with smaller loads.

It was hard, discouraging work, especially when he shoveled a clear space, and the mud came oozing back almost as quickly. He thrust his shovel into the ground and leaned on the handle, breathing heavily. He looked at Seth and James. They weren't making any more progress than he was. Someone walking on the scene would hardly know they'd been working for the better part of an hour. Josh wanted to swear. It was a losing battle.

He threw his shovel to the side. They'd be lucky to get the stage out; there was no way they'd get this road cleared until it had dried out a far sight more than it was now.

He'd have to look at the Oregon Express's books when he got home. He'd been putting it off, hoping they could get the road opened.

"We could be at this all day and still not make much more progress." Seth leaned on his own shovel.

"Yeah, that's what I was thinking. Should we see if we can

get the coach out?" Josh wiped his sleeve across his brow, sweating despite the coolness of the day.

"Might as well. I'll go get the horses."

Josh nodded. His mind ran through all possible options to save his company. He still had the mail contract. If he could get some mules, he could deliver the mail and some supplies.

If he could get some mules.

Seth led the two stage horses. They didn't like the mud any better than the men did, and their reluctance made his job harder.

Josh trudged over to help. He called back over his shoulder. "Hey, James? See if you can scrounge up some branches we can put under the wheels."

James nodded and tromped off to pick up branches swept across the road with the mud.

Seth and Josh worked on harnessing the stage horses to the coach. He'd thought two horses would be enough to pull an empty coach free, but now he wasn't so sure.

He checked the harnesses on the horses and the hitch, and then he and Seth joined James in finding branches and shoving them in front of the wheels. When each wheel had something solid to roll up on, Josh climbed up to the driver's seat and took the reins, while Seth attempted to loosen the mud around each of the wheels. Then he and James trudged to the back of the stage.

"Ready?" Josh called.

"Yep."

Josh slapped the ribbons and yelled to the horses while James and Seth pushed. The stage didn't budge for several moments then rocked slightly.

He clenched his jaw.

"Let's try it again," Seth shouted. "Maybe we loosened it up some."

As far as he was concerned, they would keep trying until the coach got free or they wore themselves out. He didn't relish the idea of leaving the coach here again, but he supposed they could come back for it with more help and more horses. If someone hadn't made it into firewood first.

"Wait a second." James leaned over and grabbed a branch. "Okay, I'm ready now."

"Hi-ya! Come on! Get up!" Josh shouted to the horses. After a long moment, the stagecoach rocked again. He risked a look down. It seemed on the verge of pulling free. *Come on!* They weren't going to lose this now. He yelled at the horses again, and after a long moment the coach pulled out of the mud with a great sucking sound. Josh encouraged the horses to keep pulling until the coach moved past the mudslide and stood on firmer ground. Once the coach was safe, Josh wrapped the reins around the brake and hopped down.

James and Seth slowly pushed themselves to their feet, covered head to toe in mud.

Josh laughed. "What happened? You couldn't resist rolling around in the mud like a couple of pigs?"

Seth tried to wipe his face but couldn't find a clean spot on his sleeve. "We were pushing against the coach when it broke free, but the mud was sucking at our boots. We couldn't get our feet under us in time."

Josh brought his laughter under control. Seth was headed his way, as fast as the mud would let him, and Josh was pretty sure he was intent on making Josh look like the two of them.

"I think there's some rags in the boot."

McKay watched as the tall girl left the barn with the younger one. The money had to be in there. Why else would she have stayed so long? As long as he'd been watching, she'd never done any outside chores. Studying the area thoroughly, he concluded no one was watching. He hurried into the barn and slipped inside. The hinges gave a brief whisper of metal on metal and then were silent.

Once inside, he waited for his eyes to adjust to the darkness. The only noise was of the animal kind. He didn't know how long he had until the men came back, so he started at the front, over by the tool bench, carefully picking things up and being careful to replace them. An old barrel held tools. He nosed around, moving handles, but didn't see anything.

He risked a peek outside the barn door. Still clear. But the thrumming of his pulse was like a clock spinning faster and faster. He hurried through the tack room and found nothing. Feeling as if someone could walk in on him at any minute, he was less careful about returning everything to its place. Order wouldn't matter if he got caught.

Nothing! He glanced up to the hay loft. That would be a good hiding spot, but unless he had several days, he'd never be able to look through all of that. He'd have to follow her and get her to tell him where she hid the money.

He'd be a lot gentler than Dillon would be.

Chapter Seven

Emily dodged a few sprinkles on the way to Parsons Hotel. The gray skies were threatening, but they were holding for now. As long as she could get to the hotel without looking like a drowned rat, she'd be happy.

For once, her luck held, and she pulled open the doors to the hotel.

Mr. Parsons was behind the desk. He glanced up when she walked in, gave her a tight smile, then returned to something on the desk.

She stepped to the desk and waited for him to look up.

He kept writing.

He saw her walk up, so what was so important that he couldn't acknowledge her? She cleared her throat.

"What can I help you with, Miss Stanton?" He didn't look up, his pen scratching across the leather-bound book on the desk.

She twisted her fingers together. "I came to speak to you about the teaching position. I'm ready to start. I have lesson plans—"

He came around the desk and grasped her elbow, pulling her along into the parlor. "Miss Stanton, you were gone an exceedingly long time. My daughter, Cassandra—as Mrs. Parsons was saying yesterday—did an admirable job in your absence. I only wish we had allowed her to teach sooner."

"Yes, I heard—" She lightly tugged at her arm, still in his firm grasp.

"She had a magnificent idea of a Valentine's Day box supper that raised money for that new school and church building, which you were fortunate to attend on Sunday."

"Oh, I—"

He released her arm and crossed his hands behind his back, tipping slightly on his toes. "There is even a small teacher's cottage that the board acquired from a poor soul who managed to make it all the way across the Oregon Trail but left after one winter." He leaned forward conspiratorially. "Cassandra and Sy used it as their home before leaving for Willamette University."

She raised her eyebrows and nodded, deciding not to attempt to speak until he'd said his fill.

"You should know, Miss Stanton, that the board was concerned by your extended absence. Ads have been placed and as soon as a suitable teacher can be found…"

She opened her mouth and closed it. She had mailed them letters informing them of her plans. Obviously Silas had intercepted them. Had he kept letters from Thomas from her as well?

"So you see, my hands are tied. You are certainly welcome to begin school on Monday, but your employment is only until a more qualified—and more dependable—teacher can be found."

Her head swam. First Thomas, and now the teaching position. Her plans were quickly slipping from her grasp. And she could not allow that to happen. The alternative was… well, it was not to be thought of.

"You will be ready, Miss Stanton, won't you?"

She straightened her spine. "Of course." She would prove *she* was the more qualified teacher, no matter who came.

JOSH POKED AT HIS PLATE. He should be hungry after all the hard work they'd put in today, but he didn't feel like eating. He was glad they'd gotten the stage out. That was one worry off his mind. But he'd hoped the road would be in better shape with a little effort.

He studied Emily. She wouldn't meet his gaze. Instead, she concentrated on her food. Something was bothering her. He wished she would tell him so he could help. Though, why should she? He couldn't even help himself much these days.

Maggie passed a basket of flaky biscuits. "Josh, how did you boys find the road today?"

He put one on his plate and took a bite, but it didn't taste much better than the mud he'd fought today.

Emily shot Maggie a small smile. What was that about?

He pushed his food around. It didn't look like he'd eaten much, and Maggie would be asking questions about that. "The mud's a good six feet thick in places and wet and heavy. In other places, the road that's left isn't wide enough for a stagecoach. We were lucky to be able to get the coach out.

"Once the road has a few days to dry out, we'll try again. Don't know when that will be since the rain started again. But the logging camp won't be up to full speed for a while yet, so some of Seth's men will help us repair the road when we can. Even with good weather, it'll take at least two weeks." He looked back at his plate and pushed his food around some more.

Maggie reached over and patted his hand.

He gave her a weak smile.

"I'll be leaving day after tomorrow to go buy a pack of mules from Jones. I have the mail contract. That will help keeps things afloat until the stage runs again." He put his fork down and pushed his plate away. "Was there anyone doing anything in the barn today? I noticed some tools out of place and the tack room was a mess." He looked around the table. He truly hoped someone had been out there and that the barn hadn't just suffered the same fate that the boardinghouse had the day before.

Emily's gaze darted to Sally before returning to her lap.

Sally spoke up. "Ma sent me to get some rags. Emily helped me. We were in the tack room—that's where we found the rags —but we didn't touch nothin.' I mean, anything. We didn't touch anything." She gave Emily a shy smile.

Emily nodded and smiled back. When she turned toward him, her smile disappeared. "My carpetbag is gone. I was looking for it, to see if it had dried. I didn't know if someone had moved it, but it's not where I left it in the barn."

A sigh pushed past his lips. He didn't need the uncertainty of a drifter, if that's what it was, while he was gone. But he had to go get the mules. "James, you keep a look out while I'm gone. I'll have another conversation with Sheriff Riley. Ladies, please be careful. Maggie—"

He looked up as Emily's chair scraped back from the table.

"Excuse me." She tossed her napkin on the table and left the room. Her footsteps sounded on the stairs follow by the sound of her door firmly shutting.

As TIRED AS HE WAS, Josh tossed and turned all night, his mind turning over the issue of the missing carpetbag, the supposed drifter, and why Emily left the supper table so suddenly.

When the first bit of pink touched the gray sky outside his window, he threw off the covers and started his day. It'd be more useful to be doing something rather than lying in bed pondering things he'd never know the answers to.

He moved to start a pot of coffee then reconsidered. Riley was an early riser. Josh could get breakfast out of him and discuss the whole situation. Maybe he'd have some insight. Regardless, he'd feel better knowing someone else shared his concerns and would keep an eye out while he was gone.

As he suspected, the smell of ham greeted him when Riley opened the door, and a few minutes later, he had a cup of coffee and a plate of ham and eggs in front of him. Once the plates were nearly clean, he updated Riley on the disappearance of Emily's carpetbag and the state of the tack room.

Riley scratched his chin. "I'm as perplexed as you are. Parsons doesn't have anyone at his hotel that looks to be a likely suspect. Not that a drifter could afford a hotel anyway. Certainly there are other more valuable things in your barn, like tools and tack, someone would take if they were looking for some quick money. Is it possible Emily's just overwrought given all that she's been through lately? Maybe she just misplaced it?"

"It's possible. After all, it's just a carpetbag. But that doesn't explain the ransacking of the house and the barn. It's like someone was looking for something. I find it hard to believe it was an old carpetbag."

Riley nodded. "Unless they thought the bag had something valuable in it."

"In which case they'd be greatly mistaken. Emily doesn't own hardly a thing, and what she does have has just about used up its usefulness." Her clothes were neat and well made, but they had clearly seen a lot of wear, and she only had a few garments. He wished there were some way to help her. But once she started teaching, she'd have a bit of money of her own.

"I'll look through the wanted posters and wires to see if there's anything there. Maybe there's a carpetbag thief on the loose."

They laughed. He thanked Riley for breakfast and headed over to Fulton's to pick up a couple of locks. But his gaze snagged on a set of new planes sitting among the tools. He picked up a beading plane, the solid weight of the wood block firm in his hand. If he had time to do more woodworking, this would fit nicely in his collection. His mind drifted to Pa. He set the plane down with more force than necessary, grabbed the locks, and headed to the counter.

Mrs. Fulton clucked her tongue. "I guess we're not the little town we used to be with all these strangers coming in. We should all be locking our doors, I suppose. I'll ask Mr. Fulton to put in another order since you grabbed our last two."

"I'd like to think we could still trust our neighbors. But with the goings on at the boardinghouse, I'd feel safer if they could lock themselves in." He didn't bother to fill her in. Being the center of the town's happenings, she always knew what was going on. "Have you seen or heard of any strange people coming through town? Anyone suspicious?"

"Now you know I'd head straight to Sheriff Riley if I saw or heard of anything. But you just never can tell with people. Why I was reading a novel about this man who was so handsome and dressed so finely. He purported to be a fine businessman, but he swindled nearly everyone out of their last dime. And it was based on a true story."

He nodded. McCormick had been well regarded last summer until his deeds became known and he tried to burn down Seth's logging camp and almost took out the town. "I'm sure Sheriff Riley appreciates your observations." He smiled, grabbed the locks, and left.

At Maggie's, he retrieved his tools from the barn and settled down next to the front door, a biscuit and a cup of hot coffee in reach. Maggie couldn't help herself; she had to feed people.

As he worked the old knob off, he wondered where Emily was. He was fitting the new lock in, trying to hold it in place while grabbing those tiny screws.

Footsteps came down the stairs behind him.

"Could you give me a hand? I need that screwdriver."

"Here you go." Emily's soft voice floated over his shoulder as the screwdriver appeared in his line of vision.

"Thanks. Could you hold this piece here?"

She reached for the lock and held it in place so he could use both hands to get the screws in the right slots. Now that she was here, he wanted to say something to reassure her, make her feel safe while he was gone. But he had no idea what.

"Um, I hope these locks help you feel more secure. You all should lock them every night. Maggie has the shotgun in her room. I talked to Riley, and he'll be looking out for you as well. Even Mrs. Fulton is keeping her eyes open for someone suspicious." Why did he say that? Like the town busybody was supposed to make Emily feel safer.

"I see." She paused. "I'm sure we'll be just fine while you're gone."

He tightened the last screw and scrambled to his feet. "Would you help me with the lock for the back door? It goes a lot faster with another pair of hands."

She nodded, and they moved to the back of the boarding-house. They worked in silence for a bit, then he tried again.

"You left the supper table early last night. Were you upset about something?"

She didn't say anything, so he plowed on. "I hope that you know you can trust all of us. We want to help. If anything is bothering you. That we could help with." Well that was eloquent. He should stick to talking to horses.

"Thank you. I do appreciate that. Actually—" She shifted her weight. "There is something maybe—"

He kept working, hoping she'd say whatever she needed to say.

"Do you need my help anymore? Because there's a letter I need you to take with you, and I still need to write it."

Before he could respond, she gathered her skirts as she passed by him and fled upstairs.

EMILY SAT at a small writing desk in her room, pen poised, but words wouldn't come. All she'd wanted to say to Silas the past week seemed frozen in her head. She could only think of Josh leaving tomorrow at dawn. If all went well, he would be back late the next day. Despite the locks and the sheriff checking on them, she was a little afraid. They still didn't know who had been in the boardinghouse and barn. Would they be safe without Josh here? Was she putting Maggie, Sally, and James in danger too?

Shaking her head, she turned her attention to the paper. There was no way to know anything for certain other than she had to get this letter written today. *Just start at the beginning.* Dipping the nib in the inkwell, she began writing.

After pouring out her anger and disappointment for nearly a page, she lifted her pen. How was she going to get the money back to Silas? She had been concentrating so much on getting a letter to him she never considered that actual method of rectifying the situation. Each day increased the chance someone would find the money, and her life as she knew it would be over. There would be no convincing Mr. Parsons she was a qualified teacher if the money was discovered. It didn't bear thinking about.

She thought for a moment and began writing again.

I believe the best solution is for you to come to Reedsville as soon as possible to retrieve the money. While the stagecoach line isn't running, you can ride as far as Oregon City and travel the rest of the way on horseback. With school starting next week, there is no way for me to get to you and this situation cannot possibly remain any longer.

Letter written, she blotted and folded it. She needed to work on her lesson plans for next week, and she had left her materials in the parlor.

She grabbed the letter and hurried down the stairs and into the parlor, putting her letter on the hall table to give to Josh.

Maggie mended while Sally worked on making quilt blocks from Maggie's scrap bag.

Emily never had the patience for needlework. She peered out the front window before gathering her books.

"With all the excitement about the men bringing the coach back yesterday, I forgot to tell you about my meeting with Mr. Parsons." Emily relayed what happened while Maggie pulled thread through a patch on James's pants.

Maggie bit off the thread. "I've seen that cottage. It needs a bit of work, but nothing that can't be handled. Josh can fix anything that needs fixing when he gets back." She folded the pants. "But you should move in there right away. You're the schoolmarm, you should live in the schoolmarm's cottage. And it'll be harder to move you out once you're settled in there." Maggie winked. "Not that I don't enjoy having you around. You're always welcome to stay here. But the more the school board sees you acting as the teacher, the harder it'll be to get you to leave."

Warmth flooded Emily's chest. No one had made her feel so welcome since Mrs. Luke. Maybe she could confide in Maggie. She had always treated Emily well and welcomed her into the group of people Maggie collected like a mother hen collects chicks.

But if Silas came to get the money, then there would be nothing to confide. She peered out the window again, as if she could see who was out there looking for the money.

Maggie put away her mending "Go look at the cottage now. You can see what needs to be done. Maybe you and I could do any cleaning that needs doing tomorrow, and Josh can make any repairs when he gets back."

Emily let the curtain fall. "Good idea." Once out the boardinghouse back door, she noticed how much the stream had swollen over its banks. The footbridge had only the ends poking out of the muddy water. Past the barn, there was a better footbridge leading to Josh's cabin. Logs had been cut in varying heights to form steps which raised the footbridge several feet above the stream.

She rounded the boardinghouse and headed toward the schoolhouse. Maggie had said she'd see the cottage set off a little ways. Not wanting to run into anyone, she stepped off the road. But after a few minutes, the grass came almost to her knees in some places, soaking her skirt, threatening to hobble her. The thick mud sucked at her boots with each step, and the hem of her skirt was already gooey. She tucked a strand of hair behind her ear and plodded on.

After visiting the cottage, maybe she'd pay a visit to Becca if the rain held off. Even if she lived in the opposite direction.

By the time she spied the schoolhouse spire, her skirt felt lined with lead. Not exactly an outfit to go calling in.

The wind picked up, chilling her. She wished she'd thought to bring a shawl. She'd walk faster to keep warm. But the sun disappeared completely behind the clouds, the air cooling faster than she could generate warmth. Fat raindrops splattered her head and shoulders.

Now would be a good time to go back. But the boarding-house was a fair bit away, and she'd certainly get soaked. She ducked into the woods that lined the road. The dense pines provided an adequate shelter, provided she didn't dislodge a branch and get showered with drops. The rain released a musty, vanilla scent. She breathed in deeply. If she weren't so cold, this would be a pleasant way to watch the rain. She could wait here a moment to see if the shower would pass quickly.

A flash of light jolted her. Instinctively, she covered her ears for the crash to follow. Her heart pounded, and her hands shook. At the next flash she huddled down at the base of the tree. A band of fear tightened around her chest. She had to get back to the boardinghouse. Being under a tree wasn't safe during a thunderstorm, and going to the cottage was no longer an option. She jumped at the next roar, shaking uncontrollably. She had to leave, but her legs were paralyzed, rooted to the ground as firmly as the tree she cowered under.

Lord, please help me. I know You haven't given me a spirit of fear, but right now I'm afraid. Help me get home.

She trembled through one more clap of thunder then sprang from under the covering of the trees and onto the road, running for the boardinghouse before she could think about what she was doing and change her mind.

She hunched over, looking at the ground, and focused on getting home before the next bolt of lightning.

Movement caught the corner of her eye. She raised her head and nearly collided with Josh's horse.

JOSH WATCHED Emily dart from the trees and run toward him. Her head was down, not paying attention to where she was going. She wouldn't see him, and she couldn't hear him through the downpour. He reined his mount to a stop. She looked up and stopped just before she ran into his horse.

Tucking a strand of wet hair behind her ear, she took a step back. "Oh, hello, Josh. I didn't know you were out here. I was just going for a walk." She rubbed her arms with her hands.

He lifted his eyebrows. "In the rain?"

"Yes. Well, no, it didn't start out that way. It wasn't raining when I left."

He reached his gloved hand down to her. "Get on up."

She took a step back. "I'm fine. I'll just walk back."

"Don't be ridiculous. You're cold and wet."

Water dripped from her hair. The rain and wind plastered her dress against her. He kept his gaze trained on her face instead of on her figure which could entice a man's thoughts into directions it shouldn't go. He couldn't believe she was refusing a ride. Did she think he could just leave her there? Especially after Maggie had sent him after her. Or did independent women have to do everything for themselves, even when it was plain stupid?

Lightning flashed in the distance, and she jumped. She took one look at his hand before grabbing it.

He pulled her up in front of him. Something hot shot through his body at her touch.

He headed them back to the boardinghouse. His arm bumped her shoulder as he held the reins, and she trembled. Lightning flared, and she pressed against him, shooting more heat through him. When the thunder followed, she hunched over and covered her ears with her hands.

Josh searched the sky. The lightning was over the mountains, nowhere near them.

Emily lowered her hands but still cowered against him, shaking.

He instinctively tightened his hold around her, ignoring the warmth flooding his limbs.

"Emily? What's the matter?"

She shook her head and tried to move away from him, but he wouldn't loosen his grip. Another round of lightning sent her back up against him.

"Are you afraid of lightning?"

She glanced at him over her shoulder and started to shake her head, but her quivering lip gave her away. She turned back. "Don't tell anyone. No one knows."

Josh grinned, glad she couldn't see him. He didn't believe for a minute no one knew she was afraid of lightning. It wasn't as if she could hide her obvious fear. Why did she think no one knew? "What do you do during lightning storms then?"

She looked over her shoulder, and Josh hid his smile. "I tell everyone I'm going to my room to read, and I put my pillow over my head."

"And they don't suspect a thing?"

"No. Why would they?"

Josh clenched his jaw to keep from laughing, but he couldn't answer her. She turned forward for a moment before looking back at him again.

"You won't tell anyone, will you?" Her eyes were wide, pleading.

"Never." The warmth in his chest grew. He liked the idea of sharing a secret with her.

"Thank you." She leaned against him, already tensed for the next round.

He shook his head and urged his horse on.

Chapter Eight

I s the water warm enough?" Maggie stood next to the stove, kettle poised, while Emily stuck her hand in the washtub.

"It's perfect. Thank you."

"You soak until you're warm through. I never should have sent you out to the cottage." Maggie pulled the kitchen curtains tightly closed.

"It's my fault. I should have looked at the sky before going so far." Emily started undoing her buttons.

"And don't sit in there after the water gets cold. You'll catch a chill." Maggie left the kitchen, pulling the door firmly shut behind her.

Emily peeled off her wet clothes and stepped into the steaming bath with relief. The water warmed her more quickly than the cup of tea Maggie had given her while they waited for the bathwater to heat.

The tub was too small to get all of herself warm at once, so she soaped and soaked each part in turn. Maggie had James put the tub close to the stove to keep Emily from getting chilled.

Finally, she was getting warmed all the way through and the heat was making her sleepy. She should hurry and finish up so Maggie could get supper on the table, but couldn't seem to make herself move any faster. Leaning against the edge of the tub, she enjoyed a few more moments of warmth before washing her hair.

The kitchen door behind her opened.

"Sorry I'm taking so long, Maggie. I just have to—" Emily turned her head, but it wasn't Maggie in the doorway.

It was Josh.

ALL JOSH WANTED WAS a hot cup of coffee. After rubbing down his horse and changing out of his own wet clothes, a cup of coffee seemed just the thing to warm him inside. Maggie always had a hot stove and a pot on. His cold stove would take too long to heat up.

Swinging open the kitchen door—why was it closed?—he rooted to the floor.

Someone was taking a bath.

Emily.

All he could see was the back of her wet head and her knees poking up out of the water. Then she turned her head. Her eyes widened and her mouth rounded as she tried to get words out. She had been expecting Maggie.

"Josh!"

Her insistent tone loosed his feet. "Oh, sorry. What are you doing taking a bath in the middle of the day anyway? It isn't even Saturday." He stepped outside, slamming the door on the last of his words.

EMILY GRABBED her brush off the dresser and picked up her damp towel. Her hair would dry faster if she sat in front of the fireplace and brushed it. She used the towel to squeeze out the last of the water out of her hair.

She still couldn't believe Josh walked in on her taking a bath. This was turning out to be a most humiliating day. She was beginning to understand why he wasn't married yet. He had the most annoying habit of seeing her at her worst. He couldn't leave well enough alone and let her walk back to the boardinghouse, so now he, of all the people in the world, knew about her secret fear. And then to walk in on her bath. It was just too much.

Though she had to admit, he got her back to the house faster than if she had walked. And it was comforting to have him behind her during the lightning. With his broad chest to lean against and his strong arm around her, she had felt protected.

Her cheeks heated. Had she done that? Had she leaned against his chest? She closed her eyes, remembering. She had.

She hung the towel over the end of the washstand and left her room. Downstairs, she turned the corner into the parlor and ran straight into Josh.

His hands went around her arms to steady her.

Her face grew hot. She squirmed and shook off his touch.

"Emily, about earlier—"

"Don't, Josh. There's nothing to talk about."

"I wanted to tell you I'm sorry. I didn't mean to walk in on you. I didn't know you were in there. I was looking for some coffee to get warmed up."

She raised her eyes to his soft brown ones. Why had she never noticed what a pretty shade of brown they were? Her heart softened. Of course he didn't walk in on her on purpose. He had to be a chilled as she was. "I forgive you." She looked past his shoulder. "Now, may I please get by?"

He stared at her for a long moment before stepping aside.

JOSH SIPPED his coffee in the parlor. He was avoiding the kitchen. He didn't need any more surprises today.

And Emily had been full of them. Seeing her on the road in

the rain, her clothes plastered against her body and then later in the tub, bare knees and the back of her head— He didn't know what to think. She had always been Thomas's in his mind, so he treated her that way. But Thomas was gone, and Emily was certainly a beautiful woman.

It had always been him, Thomas, and Seth. Just the three of them making their way. He had never pictured the future any different. And now Thomas was dead, and Seth was married. He could admit to himself that he found more excuses to be at Maggie's so he could avoid the emptiness of his own cabin. With Emily staying at Maggie's until she could return to the teacher's cottage, he had even more reasons to hang around.

He swirled the last of the coffee in his mug. He needed a refill but wasn't about to go back into the kitchen. Instead, he swallowed the last bit and stretched out his legs, easing the kinks caused by the cold and today's exertions. He'd thoroughly cleaned the stagecoach from its journey through the mud. He'd come into the boardinghouse, planning to head out to see Sheriff Riley, just to have Maggie send him to look for Emily.

That warm spot in his chest grew at being able to help Emily and protect her. But cold reality doused it. The Oregon Express wouldn't be running until that road was cleared. While he had some money saved and lived simply, he was looking at an uncertain future. Seth had almost been brought to ruin last summer. Josh had helped him out by putting up the Oregon Express as collateral so Seth could keep the logging camp afloat. They'd nearly paid back all the loans, but it still hung over his head. And he didn't want Seth to know how it worried him.

Not to mention he had a drunk for a father. Something only Seth had seen up close, though Maggie knew. In the way that only she seemed to now things. A woman like Emily was far too refined and educated for the likes of him. He hardly went to school himself, preferring to fish or hunt to put food on the table when he wasn't dragging his father out of a bar.

He shook his head. It wasn't like him to dwell on such

things. As soon as the rain stopped, they'd take another shot at clearing the road. Emily would move into the teacher's cottage, and there wouldn't be much reason to see each other.

Sally stepped into the room. "Mama says supper's ready."

He wasn't hungry.

Chapter Nine

The sky above the mountains was just turning pink as Josh led his two horses out of the barn. The air was cold, and the only clouds were the ones his breath made. Slogging footsteps through the still-soggy yard caused him to look up.

Seth raised a hand in greeting. When he was close enough, he said, "You ready to go?"

"Yep. I brought extra supplies in case I run into any trouble, but otherwise I hope to be home late Friday. Thanks for keeping an eye on things while I'm gone. I talked to Mike Riley, and he'll keep an eye out as well."

"No problem. I'm finished with the designs for the logging camp buildings and made a few improvements. When you get back, I'll start rebuilding."

Josh nodded. "Nobody's been hurt, so maybe there's no real danger, but I don't want to take any chances. And Emily has a habit of taking walks at the worst possible time." He ran his hands over the tack, examining it and checking the fastenings.

"I'll see if she wants to visit Becca. Becca's been feeling a little under the weather lately and could use the company."

"Must be something going around. I woke up with a scratchy throat this morning." He felt Seth's eyes on him as he checked the horses. "Go ahead and say what you want to say. We've been friends long enough."

Seth chuckled. "It's none of my business, just idle curiosity about you and Emily."

He finished his inspection before speaking. "She needs looking after."

"You never seemed to think so before."

"Thomas was here before."

Josh tied up the horses, and he and Seth walked into the kitchen. Its warmth felt good after the chilly morning air.

Maggie handed them each a cup of coffee and pointed to a bulging flour sack on the table. "I packed you some biscuits and a few other things. Can't travel on an empty stomach."

"Thanks, Maggie."

The room grew quiet as the men finished their coffee, and Maggie busied herself.

He looked up as Emily came in. He hid his smile, but his chest felt lighter. She was still bleary eyed and hadn't put up her hair. It must take her awhile to wake up. She looked sweet, but he didn't think she'd see it that way. "Good morning. I didn't think I'd see you before I left."

"I had to come say goodbye." She moved to the stove and poured herself coffee.

He glanced at Seth and found him fighting a smile, eyebrows raised.

Josh shook his head slightly and downed the last of his coffee. "I'd better get going." He set down his cup and grabbed his hat.

Seth went out the kitchen door as Josh picked up the flour sack. "Thanks again, Maggie." He gave her a hug.

"You be careful now," she said.

He nodded, then looked at Emily.

"I'll come outside with you."

They walked out the back door. Seth had untied the horses and was holding them near the porch steps.

Josh walked down the steps, put the flour sack in his saddle-bag, and turned around.

Emily followed him down the steps. The first light of the day played across her hair, making it almost silvery.

"Be careful while I'm gone. Seth said he'd take you over to see Becca if you felt the need to get out of the house. Even if you're going to Fulton's, take James with you. I'll check out the teacher's cottage with you when I get back."

"You be careful too."

"I plan on it." He held her gaze. She looked so vulnerable. His eyes flicked to her hair, and he reached out to touch a curl that fell over her shoulder. It felt as silky as it looked.

Emily took a step, closing the distance between them.

His arms went around her, and he pulled her to him. Her arms were around his waist and her head tucked under his chin. A soft scent, like wildflowers, surrounded him.

She pulled back, breaking the embrace, and ran up the stairs. "Goodbye." It was barely more than a whisper tossed over her shoulder before she was through the kitchen door. It slammed shut behind her.

Her warmth left him, leaving behind a strange sense of loss. He stared at the kitchen door for a moment before turning to his horse.

Seth handed him the reins, openly grinning.

Josh had forgotten he was there. He ignored the silly grin and swung up into the saddle.

"Have a safe trip."

He nodded and nudged his horse forward, sending them out on Main Street and the beginning of their journey. He'd have plenty of time to contemplate Miss Emily Stanton.

EMILY HEADED UPSTAIRS TO strip the sheets from the beds and gather the dirty clothes. Maggie set the washtub on the back porch and put the kettle on to boil. It wasn't Monday, the usual washday, but since the sun was shining today, it had to be done. The mud created more laundry than usual.

Laundry was her least favorite chore. It was hard work, and her back and arms always ached the next day. Having done enough of it over the years, she learned to be good at it and get through it quickly, but she never liked it. Or the memories that relentlessly floated to the top like soap bubbles, faster than she could pop them.

When she realized what she and Silas were doing was really stealing, she confessed and did nearly the whole town's washing to make reparations. But her confrontation with the man she thought was her grandfather had changed things between them forever.

"I'm not helping you anymore." She had stormed away from the wagon after folding and packing in the last load of laundry.

"It's just harmless fun. Besides, we gots to eat, child. What's so wrong in having a few extras with our meal?" Grandfather's laugh turned her stomach like the time he'd given her those sweet candies and she'd eaten them all.

She knew what they were doing was wrong, but what could she do? She'd seen the street children who were on their own. Rag-clothed thin bodies and dirty faces held empty, hopeless eyes. "No, it's not. It's stealing."

"Them folks can afford it."

"That doesn't make it right."

"How they treated you, was that right?"

She stopped, deflated. Tears burned her eyes. She turned away so Grandfather couldn't see. "No."

She tossed the wash water on the grass and winced as the water sloshed on her hand, burning the raw skin. She hooked the washbasin on the side of the wagon and then went to the back and rummaged for some salve to put on her hands.

"Let me do that." Grandfather's greater height allowed him a better view of the wagon's contents. He withdrew a jar and opened it.

When she reached for it, he took her hand and began rubbing the salve into the raw skin. He finished and wordlessly handed her the jar. "Let's get moving."

"Here's the last of them." Maggie's voice pulled her from her memories. A pile of sheets landed at her feet.

Emily brought her mind back to the present. She scooped up the pile. Once outside, she and Maggie worked in companionable silence as the memories slowly faded. But the pain and fear she felt as a twelve-year-old girl lingered.

Time to think of something else. Scrubbing a stained shirt on the washboard, she thought back to this morning and her cheeks heated. With a furtive glance, she saw Maggie using a broomstick to stir the whites boiling in the copper pot.

She wasn't sure whether she'd flown into Josh's arms, or he'd pulled her into his. She hoped he didn't think she was overly forward. But his arms had tightened around her, and he had stroked her hair. Only her acute embarrassment at realizing Seth was watching them had driven her into the house.

She tossed the shirt into the rinse water. It wasn't very ladylike to hug a man in the yard. She couldn't help the smile that crept out; being in Josh's arms had been wonderful. It tugged out the faded feeling that surfaced when she saw a family where the parents and children laughed and cared for each other in a way that radiated security and love. Something she'd only witnessed from the outside.

Trying to recapture that feeling of security, she replayed the embrace in her mind. What did Josh think? Could he possibly have feelings for her? Or did he simply feel responsible for her safety? Still, the way he'd held her... She shook her head. It didn't matter. Until that money got back to Silas, she couldn't move on with her life. And if her memories taught her anything, it was that people would still scorn you when you tried to do the right thing.

Thinking of the money made her scan the yard and the nearby grove. Maggie was nearby, and James had turned out the horses into the corral and was working in the barn. Maybe the man had given up and moved on after taking her carpetbag.

She tossed the last of the rinsed clothes into the basket and moved to the clothesline. As she pinned up the garments, something caught her eye past the yard, toward the edge of the woods. She stilled, her mind trying to make sense of what she saw.

A man ducked behind a tree.

JOSH SHOULD HAVE FELT MORE relieved to reach the livery in Oregon City than he did. Thankful for good weather on the trip, he couldn't pinpoint his source of unease. He supposed it was worry about Emily. Though Seth and Riley would keep an eye on her, they had other responsibilities. And he had to get the mules and keep delivering the mail if he wanted to keep things afloat.

He had surprised himself when he'd pulled her into his arms this morning, hadn't even known he was going to do it until he was holding her. It was like holding a foal, she was so small and delicate. The urge to protect her was so strong he didn't want to leave.

It ended too soon. She had rushed out of his arms and into the house. What was he thinking being so forward?

And yet, she had hugged him back.

He coughed, a sharp pain stabbing his ribs, adding to his overall achy feeling. Discontent nipping at his heels, he switched horses and got directions to Jones's mule ranch. But there was one thing he wanted to take care of and he had to do it now.

Making sure no one was watching, he pulled out a leather pouch from his saddlebag. He had taken all the money out of the safe in the barn floor. He opened the pouch and removed a few bills, stuffing them in his pocket, then slipped the pouch down the front of his shirt. Strolling out of the livery, the bright sunlight stung until his eyes adjusted. He headed up the street toward the mercantile.

A bell tinkled above the door as he opened it and stepped inside. This mercantile was a far sight bigger than Fulton's, something Josh was counting on. There were a few things he needed to get.

As he browsed the aisles, looking for what was on his list, he also hoped to spot something that wasn't on his list. His mind drifted to Emily. She'd had such a rough time of it lately, he wanted to see her smile.

Both of the store's clerks were busy with other customers, and Josh was just as glad. He wanted some time to look without pressure. Stopping at the selection of books, he ran a finger along their spines, certain one of them would please her. The question was, which one? What if he got her one she owned, or had already read?

And then he remembered. They had been discussing Mr. Twain's adventures at supper one night. She had mentioned reading his book, *Innocents Abroad* and wishing she could get his latest one, *Roughing It.* There it was. He slid it off the shelf and added it to his pile, feeling like a weight had lifted. A weight he'd been carrying since he left Reedsville.

He approached the counter where the now-free clerk smiled at him. Something snagged his attention out of the corner of his eye. Now that would be perfect for Emily. He debated with himself for only a moment and then snapped it up. One gift might be seen as friendship, but two? He refused to think about what it might mean.

A moment later, he whistled as he walked back to the livery, despite the clouds that had gathered overhead blocking out the last of the day's sun.

EMILY PASSED a basket of Maggie's flaky biscuits to Sheriff Riley.

"Can't resist Maggie's biscuits." He put one on his plate and began to butter it. After he'd come out to check on the man Emily had seen in the woods, Maggie had insisted he stay for supper.

He'd found some broken branches and trampled grass that proved someone had been there. So Emily hadn't imagined it. She had wondered momentarily if the strain of the situation was making her see things.

But he hadn't been able to find where the man went. "If Josh was here, he'd be able to track him, most likely. I'm just not as good at tracking as he is. Don't know anyone who is."

Emily wondered if Josh had arrived at his destination and if the weather had been good for him. He would never admit it, but the muddy roads weighed on him. She could see it, almost an invisible burden on his shoulders. He had to get the Oregon Express up and running. She didn't know for sure, but she imagined it being out of commission created a financial strain. She thought of the money hidden behind the manger. It was too bad it couldn't be used to help.

"Don't you agree, Emily?"

She looked up. What had she missed? "I'm sorry, Maggie. Woolgathering."

"I was just telling Mike here how nice it was to do the laundry in the sunshine and enjoy it a bit today." Maggie's eyes twinkled.

Did her thoughts show? She sometimes wondered if Maggie could read her mind. "Um, yes. The sun was enjoyable." Laundry, though, never would be. She turned to the sheriff. "How was your day? Before you tried to track our mystery man."

His eyes slid to the side, and then he cleared his throat. "I was just telling Maggie about Bill Benchly's latest scheme."

"Ah." Her face flooded with heat. "My thoughts really had wandered."

His eyes softened. "Understandable." He leaned back in his chair. "I would heed Josh's warnings. Don't go outside alone. It's clear the man been in that spot awhile, probably watching your comings and goings. It would make sense that he knew when you were gone to church then." He met her gaze. "If we knew what he was after, we might have a better idea of figuring out who he was."

She made sure to hold his gaze. "I was thinking that too. The best I can come up with is that he has me confused with someone else. Someone who has something valuable."

Riley nodded. "That makes sense. If I can find him, I could ask him."

If she could talk to the man, maybe she could find out what he wanted, and she could convince him that she didn't have it. Unless the money really was is. But how would she determine that? It seemed the only way would be to have a conversation with the man. As dangerous as that would be, at least it put only herself in danger. The way things were now, she was putting the entire household in danger.

Chapter Ten

Pitch dark surrounded Josh. He wasn't sure at first his eyes were open. He sat up. Where was he? Slowly, shapes formed in the darkness, and he remembered. He was in Jones's barn. He laid back, the sweet, faintly musty smell of hay surrounding him. What had woken him?

A drop of wetness thumped him on the forehead and rolled across his temple. He realized the solid background of noise was rain pounding the barn roof. A second drop hit his head. This roof had a leak, and he was right under it.

He rolled to his side, but his ribs hurt. A coughing fit seized him, which didn't help. He had hoped the cough was gone. Mrs. Jones had heard him coughing before supper and prepared him a special tea. It tasted like some herbs he couldn't identify mixed with honey. But it wasn't too bad, and it seemed to have done the trick. Until now.

He coughed again and tried to get comfortable, despite his burning throat. He and Jones had quickly come to a fair deal. They invited Josh to stay to supper and sleep in the barn. Even with the leaky roof, it beat sleeping out in the rain.

Eyes wide open, he stared at the blackness above him. Another cough was coming, and he tried to suppress it. What time was it anyway? No light shone through the cracks in the boards. Was dawn near?

Tossing aside his bedroll, he got up and cracked open the barn door. It was black as pitch outside too. No moon, no stars, just the steady downpour. He shut the door and latched it. Going back to his pile of straw, he plunked down and coughed. He closed his eyes and wrapped his bedroll tight around him, hoping he could sleep. Otherwise it would be a long time until morning.

STARING OUT HER BEDROOM WINDOW, Emily examined the spot where Sheriff Riley had figured the man had been watching them. He had a great view of her window and yet he would remain hidden by the tree branches and undergrowth.

A shiver shook her. How often had she been in front of this window? He could tell when her light went out at night. She slid along the wall where she could look outside without being seen. She watched for what felt like an eternity but never saw any movement. What did she expect? The man's hiding spot had been found. It wouldn't be likely for him to return to it.

Josh would be back tonight. Calm and anticipation settled on her in equal measures at the thought. She found she missed him. Which surprised her completely. She'd been away from Thomas for nine months, and while she thought of him frequently, it wasn't as often as Josh had invaded her thoughts in the two days he'd been gone. Instead of pondering what that might mean, she pushed it aside and concentrated on the problem at hand.

Josh wouldn't like one bit the idea of her talking to that man. If she wanted to do any exploring, now would be her only chance. She slipped out to the back yard and walked around the barn, finding a spot where she could study the woods. After seeing only movement of birds flitting from branch to limb and underbrush rustling that was most likely caused by squirrels or rabbits instead of humans, she grew bolder.

She strode to the woods and entered their shade, hiding herself from the house, but careful not to move in too deep where she couldn't dash out again if she needed to. Moving with small steps and stopping frequently, she focused on reaching the area from where the man had been spying on her.

As soon as she was close enough to see the spot, she leaned against a tree and peered around it. The spot was an even better choice than it appeared from her bedroom window. Low-hanging branches concealed it well, and a soft bed of pine needles made passing time more comfortable and deadened the sound of movement. A log had been dragged under the branches to form a seat or back rest.

Was her carpetbag around here anywhere? Surely if it were, Sheriff Riley would have found it. But he was looking for a man, not a valise. She studied the log. It had a hollow end. Maybe her bag was in there.

She glanced around and then walked over to the log. Bending over, she peered in one end. Too dark to see in very far. She grabbed a branch off the ground and poked in the end, hoping she wouldn't anger some animal that had made this log its home. Nothing but decayed wood. At the other end, she found the same thing.

Sighing, she dropped the branch. What had she hoped to find out here?

Footsteps crashing through the woods caused her heart to race. She dashed behind the tree.

"Emily! Are you out here?"

James! Maggie must have sent him looking for her. She had been gone too long. How on earth would she explain this?

Gathering her skirts, she darted out from behind the tree. "Here I am, James." With more explanations to make and no further answers, she headed to the boardinghouse as the skies opened up and started to pour.

JOSH HAD NEVER BEEN SO glad to see the boardinghouse. He couldn't remember half the trip, but it didn't matter now. He was home.

The circuit preacher, Roy Adams, had caught up with him in Oregon City and rode in with him. Which was Providence given how poorly Josh was feeling. His horse headed for the barn; Had he guided him there? He didn't know. But the barn door was closed. It took him three tries to kick his right foot out of the stirrup. His leg felt filled with lead as he swung it over the horse. Somehow, he was on the ground, standing next to his horse.

"You're home. Hey, Pastor Adams."

He turned at the voice. James stood behind him. Josh hadn't heard him approach. "Yeah."

"Why don't you go inside? I'll take care of the horses and mules. Looks like you got some good ones." James continued to stare at him, as if expecting him to do something.

He couldn't figure out what it was. Pastor Adams was grabbing the saddlebags.

"Josh, you're soaking wet. Go inside. Ma has hot broth on the stove."

He nodded and moved toward the boardinghouse, Pastor Adams with him. He trudged up the steps and pulled open the door. Everything seemed so difficult. He must be really tired. He hadn't slept much last night after the leaky roof, and his cough had awoken him. As if on cue, he began coughing violently. He couldn't even get through the kitchen door. Pastor Adams slipped an arm around him and helped him through.

"Goodness, get yourself in here." Maggie bustled around him and pushed him in the kitchen. "You're soaked to the skin. I don't know which to make you do first: get some hot food on you or get you in dry clothes."

She pulled a chair over next to the stove and Pastor Adams dropped him into it. Someone handed him a towel and he tried to sop up as much of the water out of his clothes as he could. Fabric brushed his arm and he looked up.

Emily stood there holding a quilt. Her smile warmed him more than stove. "Here, let's get this around you." She smelled fresh as she leaned forward to drape the fabric around him.

He thought of her gift in his saddlebags. James would take care of them, he was good with things like that, but Josh still wished they were in his possession.

She moved over to the stove, next to Maggie, and a moment later handed him a cup of something hot. He took a sip. Sweetened tea. It felt good going down, warming him all the way to his middle.

Maggie introduced Emily to Pastor Adams and then dished up supper. "You'll have your usual room, Pastor."

"Thanks, Maggie."

What went unspoken was that all the rooms were available because there were no stagecoach guests and no boarders.

Emily moved around the kitchen, but Josh always kept her in his line of sight. He noticed her glancing his way more than a few times.

Maggie took his empty cup and replaced it with a warm bowl of stew. When he was treated as well as this, why did he ever leave here? The tea and stew had nearly warmed him except for the chill deep in his bones. All he wanted now was dry clothes and his bed. He handed his bowl to Maggie.

"Do you want another helping?"

"No, thank you, Maggie. It was good and just what I needed, but all I want to do now is fall into bed." He stood up and took the quilt from his shoulders. Emily took it from him and folded it over her arm.

"You do that. Here." Maggie grabbed a cloth, bent down, and reached underneath the stove. She pulled out a hot brick and wrapped it the rest of the way with the cloth before handing it to him. "Put this at the foot of your bed to warm it. Don't need you to catch a chill."

"Thanks, Maggie."

"Josh, need a hand getting home?" Pastor Adams laid a beefy paw on his shoulder. The man looked like he could have been a pugilist at one time. Maybe he had been. He hadn't been real forthcoming about his past. Not many people pried, either. As he liked to say, we all are new creations in Christ. Something Josh was particularly grateful for.

"No, thanks. I can manage."

"And don't even think about getting up early to do chores. James can handle it."

He grinned and headed for the back door. He opened it and started to leave when Emily's voice stopped him.

"Josh?"

He turned.

"I'm glad you're back."

He smiled at her. "Me too."

JOSH WOKE up the next morning. The sunlight slanted in through his windows at an angle that told him he had slept far later than normal. He had a slight headache, but his cough was gone. Must have just needed a good night's rest. He didn't feel too bad.

He washed and dressed and headed down to the boardinghouse.

As he came through the back door, Maggie looked up from the stove. "Josh, I didn't expect to see you up. How are you feeling?"

"Not too bad. Probably better after coffee and breakfast."

She ushered him to the table and soon had a plate and mug in front of him.

Emily entered the kitchen with an armful of books. "Oh, Josh." She stopped. "How are you?"

Surprisingly better now that he'd seen her. He vaguely

remembered her wrapping him in a quilt last night. "Just needed a good night's sleep. Where's Pastor Adams?"

"He's out making calls to the surrounding area. He was going to stop by Seth's and see if they could get a service together for some of the loggers, whoever might still be around."

He nodded toward the books. "Working on school?" The book he'd gotten her was still in the saddlebags James had deposited at his cabin. How would he give her his gifts? He couldn't imagine doing it at the supper table with everyone looking on. Had it been a good idea at all?

She eased into a chair next to him. "Yes. It starts Monday. I've finished my lesson plans, but I keep going over them and thinking of things I could add."

He swallowed his bite. "Did you make it over to the teacher's cottage?"

"No." She glanced back at Maggie. "We thought it was best to wait until you returned."

He scraped his fork across the plate and shoved the last bite in his mouth. "We can go now."

Her face lit up and then dimmed. "But you're sick. You should rest."

"I'm fine. Just needed a good night's sleep and some of Maggie's good cooking." He stood and put on his hat. "Let's go."

EMILY STUDIED Josh studying the room. The cottage was just one room that shared a privy with the church/schoolhouse. And with Josh in it, seemed even smaller. Still, Emily had never had any place that was hers alone, not borrowed from someone or shared with someone.

He tapped the handle of the hammer on the beams then peered up at the roof.

She saw it too. Even she knew a hole in the roof wasn't a good thing.

He turned and gave her his classic grin. "It's a hole, but it's not much of a problem. Probably lost a few shingles in the last storm. But there's not much water damage." He gave a small cough.

"So you can fix it?" She squeezed the handle of the bucket of cleaning supplies.

He nodded. "I can fix it. I need a few shingles, which I don't have with me. But, I can rig something up to keep the rain out until we can get some."

His gaze met hers and heat spread across her chest and up her face. "So, um, I'll start sweeping, I suppose."

He gave his hammer a little toss. "And I'll start hammering." He rummaged around in his toolbox and then set up the ladder he'd brought with him.

After a few minutes of his hammer tapping away, he looked down. "So why did you want to become a schoolmarm?"

"I loved books. They were a wonderful way to take me to anywhere in the world. And I could learn so much from them. It seemed like the most natural thing to share that with others." It didn't do justice to how she felt, but she couldn't quite put it all into words. Not the *rightness* she felt teaching. She was someone who mattered, who could help others.

"I didn't much like school myself. Before my pa got hurt, he was a woodworker, and I'd get to help him with jobs. After he got hurt, well, I tried to keep up the jobs I could do as long as possible. When I did go to school, I'd missed so much that I'd get frustrated and then I'd rather just go fishing. Sometimes I'd get Seth to go with me."

She set her broom aside and watched him work. "Maggie said you could build or fix anything. Is your pa still alive? You mentioned he got hurt."

"Yeah. He is." But his voice was as tight as a closed door. Clearly not a subject he wanted to talk about.

She understood that. She had plenty of subjects she didn't

want to talk about either. "You're quite busy running the stage. Do you have much time to do any woodworking?"

He coughed again before he answered her. "Not as much as I'd like. But I manage to make a few Christmas gifts each year." A few more taps with his hammer, and he headed down the ladder. "What about you? What do you like to do when you're not teaching or helping Maggie? Any fancy needlework?"

She grabbed the bucket. She needed water to wash the windows. There was a pump outside. "Um, no. Just reading. Never learned to do any fancy work. Or had any time." She headed out to the pump, but Josh took the bucket from her and pumped water into it.

"I'll help you wash the windows." He carried the bucket back inside.

"Oh." She handed him a rag and dipped hers in the water. His forehead beaded with sweat, though it wasn't that warm out. Despite his claim that a good night's sleep had cured him, he was still sick. Getting to admit it seemed about as likely as pulling a mule from a feeding trough. Her only hope was to finish here quickly so he could get home and rest. Or at least she could turn Maggie loose on him.

He started on the window to the left of the door. There were only two. She started on the right one.

"Is your grandfather the only family you have left?"

Silas, she mentally corrected. "Yes. Well, no. Silas isn't exactly family. I found out recently that he's not even my grandfather, though I always thought he was. Apparently, after my parents died of some illness outbreak, my real grandfather gave me to Silas. He wasn't well himself and died soon after. Silas raised me as a granddaughter, but we're not blood." She looked sideways at Josh, gauging his reaction. She'd never told anyone about Silas, not even Mrs. Luke.

"You're fortunate your grandfather found someone to raise you and didn't leave you to be an orphan." He paused. "My ma died of consumption when I was thirteen. Seth's pa and Maggie and her husband, Stephen, when he was alive, took me under their wings and kept me out of trouble." He paused again. "My pa started drinking when he got hurt working. It got out of hand, and he wasn't around much." H scrubbed the window pane, stifling another cough.

Her heart softened at the image of Josh as a young man hurt and angry. Neither of them had had idyllic childhoods. They had a common background in pain. Maybe, just maybe, she could trust him with her secret. If anyone could understand why she did what she did, he might.

Chapter Eleven

The clouds moved back in again while Josh and Emily walked home, but the weather seemed to be holding. For Josh's sake, Emily hoped it did. Though he didn't say it, the lack of the stage runs weighed on him, slumping his shoulders. After their conversation, she felt closer to him, like they shared a bit of a bond because of their mutually difficult backgrounds.

At the boardinghouse, she thanked Josh again for his help. He waved her off and headed toward the barn before she could figure out how to get him in front of Maggie.

She'd change first and then talk to Maggie. As she dashed upstairs, one thought flooded her mind: her own cottage! She clasped her hands to her chest. It was clean and ready for her to live in. And thanks to Josh's help, the roof didn't leak. She could move her few things over tomorrow, get some supplies, and be ready for school to start on Monday.

Lifting her bedroom curtain to check the weather, she noticed it was still cloudy but not raining. She let the curtain fall from her hand but jerked it back an instant later. Her heart beat faster. She'd seen something. What was it? Studying the area behind the barn, she looked for anything out of the ordinary. No, nothing. It was just her imagination.

Except that her valise sat next to the corral, leaned up against the railing. Her hand flew to her mouth. How did that…

She didn't bother to finish the thought but tore downstairs, barely avoiding slipping in her stockings. She pulled on her boots and raced across the yard, not caring that she promptly splashed mud on her clean skirt.

Grabbing the carpetbag, she breathed hard—straining against her corset stays—while scanning the yard. Nothing seemed out of place. The area around the corral was well-trampled and any new footprints were indistinguishable. A copse of trees stood not too far from here. It would be a perfect hiding place, a new one, but if anyone waited there she couldn't spot him in the dark recess.

She opened her valise. It was empty. She half-hoped for a note or something that would clue her into whoever was out there. What did he want with her? Was he trying to tell her something? She couldn't figure it out. Dropping the bag to her side, she turned to go in.

She heard a squish of mud behind her and started to turn. A vise-like grip encircled her arm, yanking her around. Her knees went weak. She forced the panic down and tried to pay attention. This had been what she wanted, to talk to the man. She looked up into a face shaded by a hat. He had a mustache and wore work clothes. She had the strangest feeling she knew him but couldn't figure out how. He didn't look any different than most of the men in town.

"Where's the money? I don't want to hurt you. I just want the money back."

No, she didn't recognize his voice.

He shook her arm and practically pulled her off her feet. "The money. Where is it?"

So he knew about the money. Did Silas steal it from him? Her head hurt.

He shook her again.

"Stop shaking me! What money?" She heard the tight squeak

in her voice. Her control was slipping, but she needed more information before giving the bank notes to him.

He glanced at her carpetbag and back at her. "It was in your bag. I saw it. Now hand it over, and I'll leave you alone."

Her stomach felt filled with lead. How could he have seen it in her bag? Did he think she took it? To her horror, tears burned her eyes. She hated crying in front of people. She blinked furiously. What should she do? Maybe she should just give him the money and be done with it. She wouldn't have to worry about anyone else finding it, and she wouldn't have to explain it. But if it wasn't his money, she would be helping him steal it. And what about Silas? *God, please help me. What do I do?*

"Hey!"

She heard footsteps behind her but couldn't tear her eyes away from the man. "I—I don't have it. I left it in Portland."

He gave her a hard look then glanced over her shoulder. "This isn't over." He shoved her, sending her sprawling on her backside in the mud, then fled into the copse. She stared after him, unable to get to her feet.

"Emily! Are you okay?" Josh bent over her, his hand on her shoulder.

She nodded.

He held out his hand.

She started to put hers in his and realized it was muddy. She pulled it back.

"Don't worry about it." He grabbed her hand and pulled her to her feet. He held on to her a moment. "Can you get into the house by yourself?"

She nodded.

"Good. Get inside. I'm going after him."

She nodded again.

He looked at her a long moment and then turned and strode into the woods.

She made it to the porch steps and collapsed on them. She put her head in her hands.

Suddenly, she knew where she'd seen the man.

McKay huddled under a sugar pine tree. More often than he liked, a drop or two of water would find its way down his collar. The stagecoach driver hadn't followed him, he was sure. And the way the man had been coughing, McKay didn't think he'd make it too far. Still, it didn't hurt to be too careful, and this was as good a place as any to wait out the rain that had just opened up.

He didn't like being so rough with women, but ever since this situation with Dillon he found himself doing things he never thought he'd do. She seemed pretty frightened of him, and he was tempted to believe what she said. If she had the money here, he hadn't found it. But if she had left it in Portland, it would be nigh impossible to find.

Under his breath, McKay swore. He'd followed her around Portland. She had to have noticed the money in her bag when she was at the hotel. So what'd she do with it? She was a woman; she wouldn't know what to do. She'd either given it to that stagecoach driver or to the shop owner. And since the stagecoach driver was here and the money wasn't, that just left the shop owner.

He ducked out of the trees and stretched his aching legs. Best get back to camp. He had a trip to Portland to make. He had no choice. Time was running out for Dillon.

Josh had followed the man into the woods behind the boardinghouse without getting so much as a glimpse of him. Any footprints were lost on the pine needles. He scanned the area for other signs. Then he started coughing. He bent over and put his hands on his knees. If the man was anywhere near here, Josh's presence wasn't a secret now. Straightening, he gave the area a final glance and then headed for home. Sheriff Riley could take up the search. Exhaustion weakened him. His legs shook like a new foal's.

Trudging back to the boardinghouse, his eyes widened. Emily hadn't made it any farther than the porch steps. Shaking his head, he picked up his pace, strode toward the back steps, and stood over her. "Why aren't you in the house? He could have come back."

She looked up. "You didn't find him?"

"No."

"I don't think he's coming back."

"You don't know that. Go inside now. I'm going to get the sheriff."

"No! I mean, we don't really need him, do we? The man didn't hurt me or take anything. Let's not stir up trouble." Emily stood. On the porch steps, she was eye level with him. Her hands twisted in her skirt.

Too much had happened for this to be a coincidence. Something was going on, and she could be in danger. "I'm getting the sheriff unless you have something to tell me to persuade me otherwise." It was a little uncomfortable to have her grey eyes the same level as his. He liked it better when she had to look up at him.

"Do what you have to do." She turned and went into the house.

He stood there. How had he become the bad guy? He couldn't figure her out. He blew out a breath, shaking off the last surge of energy that had rushed through him when he saw that man grabbing her.

She knew more than she was telling, that was obvious. But why wouldn't she trust him? After their work on the cottage today, he thought they had a better understanding of each other. He hadn't talked about Pa with anyone in a long time. And he was certain no one knew about her past.

He walked to the barn and yanked open the door, standing

inside for a moment, not sure what to do. What he wanted to do was climb in the hay loft and take a nap. Something he hadn't done in years.

He took off his hat and jerked his fingers through his hair. Emily had him tied in knots, a feeling he didn't like at all. He was worried about her, and he didn't know what to do about that.

Shoving his hat back on, he walked out of the barn and over to the sheriff's office. Through the window he saw Mike Riley sitting behind his desk looking through wanted posters. He stepped into the office, and Mike looked up.

"Hey, Josh."

"Mike. Looks like our visitor is back. I caught him grabbing Emily out by the corral and chased him into the woods before I lost him."

Mike stood and strapped on his gun belt. "Does Emily know who it is?"

"I don't know. She's not telling me anything."

Mike looked at Josh a moment and then nodded. "Let's go see what we can find."

A moment later, the two were in Maggie's kitchen with cups of coffee. Emily sat at the kitchen table in a clean dress. She stared at the cup in her hand. He couldn't tell how the experience had affected her. He'd let Mike do the questioning since Josh had gotten nowhere.

"Emily, why don't you tell me what happened?" Mike asked.

She looked at Mike and then Josh before gazing back at her cup. "Josh and I had worked on getting the teacher's cottage ready for me to move into. I had gone upstairs to change out of my work dress when I thought I saw something from the window. When I looked closer, I saw my carpetbag by the corral. I had been looking for it the other day but couldn't find it. I wondered how it got out there, so I went to get it.

"That's when he grabbed my arm and asked me where the money was. I told him I didn't know what he was talking about, but he kept shaking me. I couldn't think of what to do, so I just blurted out that I'd left the money in Portland."

She looked at Josh. "That's when you came up, and he ran away."

"After shoving you down," he added.

She nodded. "That's why I think he won't be coming back. If he thinks the money he's looking for is in Portland, maybe he'll go back there."

"Can you describe the man for me?" Mike asked.

"He's a little shorter than Josh, with a mustache and dark eyes. Thin build. He was wearing work clothes today but, when I saw him on the ferry, he was dressed in a suit."

"You know him?" Josh's voice reverberated in the kitchen. Its volume surprised even him. He rarely raised his voice.

"I don't *know* him. When I bumped into him on the ferry, he was dressed completely differently, his mustache was waxed, and he wore too much scent, but I believe it was the same man. I tried to get around him, but he grabbed my arm the same way he did today and was overly, uh, friendly. That was all. If he'd been wearing that scent today, I would have recognized him immediately."

"Did he say 'the' money or 'your' money?" Mike asked.

Emily furrowed her brow. "'The' money, I'm fairly certain. Why?"

"I was just wondering if he thought you were wealthy, by seeing a piece of jewelry or something, and was following you to rob you. It would explain why he went through the boardinghouse."

"I see." She shook her head. "I don't have any jewelry. I was wearing my best dress on the ferry, but it certainly wouldn't make anyone think I was wealthy."

"It's your bag," Josh said.

Mike and Emily looked at him.

"Your valise. It's a fairly common one. I see ones like it all the time on the stagecoach. Maybe he's confusing it with someone else's."

Emily slowly nodded. "True. There's nothing unique about it."

Mike rubbed his chin. "Makes perfect sense to me." He leaned back in his chair. "So when would he have seen you with your bag?"

"He got off the ferry before I did." Emily shook her head. "I never saw him after that until today."

"He must have waited for you somewhere and followed you." Mike took a sip from his mug.

Emily shuddered. "I hate to think someone was following me, and I didn't know it. I didn't do much in Portland. I went straight from the ferry to the Oregon Express office and met Josh. We had supper at Josiah's, I stayed at the hotel, and then we left the next morning. If he followed me the whole time, he'll know I didn't stop at a bank. That only leaves…" She put her hand to her forehead.

"Josiah's and the Oregon Express office," Josh finished for her. She looked miserable. He knew she prided herself on her thinking. Yet her solution to get this man out of their lives just dragged someone else into it.

She dropped her hand from her forehead, and Josh reached over to squeeze it. He caught Mike's gaze from the corner of his eye and quickly moved his hand back to his cup.

Mike sat forward. "I'll telegraph Josiah to be careful and then follow with a more detailed letter."

"Do you think he'll be back?" Emily asked Mike.

"I don't know. It's possible he believed you and will go to Portland to look for the money. After all, why would you bring it here?" Mike rubbed his chin. "Still, it's strange. Where'd this money come from? Is it his or something he stole? Was someone bringing it to him in a bag like yours?" He shook his head. "The way he approached you suggests everything's not on the up and up. But I don't suppose we'll ever know."

Josh watched as Emily's delicate face seemed to sag.

Mike apparently saw it too. He caught Emily's gaze. "Don't worry. Either this fellow will give up or we'll catch him." He smiled at her.

Josh cleared his throat and stood. "Mike, let me show you where I tracked him."

Mike stopped smiling at Emily and pushed his chair back. "Let me know if you need anything."

She nodded.

Josh tightened his jaw. Mike seemed a little too interested in Emily, and she didn't need that right now.

Or maybe that's what she wanted. She hadn't told Josh anything until Mike had come over. He shoved his hat on his head and thrust open the kitchen door.

Chapter Twelve

Emily, Maggie, and Sally brought in the bowls of food and set them on the dining room table. Supper was ready. Emily started to take her seat when she felt a hand on her chair.

"Allow me."

Emily turned and found herself inches from Josh's chest. She looked up into his warm brown eyes, and the warmth spreading across her shoulders loosened them. He held her gaze until she looked away and allowed him to seat her. He was obviously trying to smooth things over, and she appreciated it.

He took the seat next to her and said the blessing. She had to talk with him tonight.

Maggie informed them that Pastor Adams was calling on folks and making the rounds. He'd have so many supper invitations that they might not see much of him. It was as if the town saved up all their spiritual needs until he came to town.

After supper, she helped Maggie and Sally with the dishes. Once the floor was swept, the table wiped down, and the dishpan emptied and hung on its nail, Emily grabbed her shawl.

"Oh, I almost forgot." Maggie's voice halted her. "A letter came for you. I picked up the mail at Fulton's today from Josh's last delivery. It's on the hall table. I didn't want you to miss it."

Silas? No, he wouldn't have received her letter and been able to send a reply in that short of time. "Thank you." She moved into the front hall and picked up the letter. Familiar script settled peace over her like a warm blanket. She'd read this tonight in bed. Tucking it into her pocket, she slipped out the kitchen door.

Light shone through gaps in the barn's wood and under the door. She pulled her shawl tightly around her and headed for the barn. Her eyes hadn't adjusted to the dark, so she crossed the yard carefully, unsure what she was going to say to Josh.

Today had been such a muddle. She hated that the sheriff had been brought into it. Josh was right to do it, but now she was deceiving one more person. Not that she had outright lied to them, she just hadn't told them everything. Like the fact that she did have the money. But soon Silas would have her letter. He would come get the money, and that would be it.

With a whoosh of metal on metal, she opened the door and entered the barn.

Josh looked up and smiled. He was sitting on a stool, saddlebags on his lap and a pile of rope, canvas, and other things she didn't recognize on the floor next to him.

Rocking back on her heels, she looked around. *Say something!* "Josh, thank you for all you did today. It's been overwhelming. Out by the corral, I just froze. I couldn't believe someone was grabbing me. Then to think he followed me all the way from the ferry... How could I not have known?" She hugged her arms across her chest.

He put the saddlebags aside and came to her, touching her arm. "Don't blame yourself. I was with you most of the time and I didn't notice anything either." He grinned. "It's not too hard to follow a stagecoach."

She gave him a small smile in return. "You're always so nice to me, trying to make me feel better."

"If Thomas were here, he'd do the same thing."

She nodded and looked away. Josh and Thomas did have a

sense of humor in common. "Thanks for being such a good friend. And fixing the roof on the cottage." She gave him a full smile. "And for keeping my secret about the thunderstorms."

He grinned. "I have something for you." He rummaged in the saddlebags and pulled out a couple of brown-paper wrapped parcels. "It's not anything really. I just saw them and thought of you." He thrust the packages at her.

She settled on a three-legged milking stool and set the packages in her lap. What on earth could he have gotten her? The first one was flat and firm. She pulled off the paper. A book. "Oh, Josh! *Roughing It* by Mr. Twain. You remembered our discussion." She held it to her chest.

He nodded, the dimple back in his cheek.

"That's so kind. Thank you. I can't wait to read it."

"There's more." He gestured to the other package. "I just thought— Well, you'll see."

This one was an odd shape. And it tinkled as she turned to open it. The paper fell away revealing a hand bell.

"Every teacher needs a bell to call the class to order. Even I know that." He grinned.

She set the parcels on the ground and jumped up to hug him. "Thank you. No one has ever been so thoughtful." She let him go and stepped quickly back, overturning the stool. Her face burned. The warmth of him had seeped through, and she could still feel its imprint on her.

His gaze was steady on hers. "You're welcome, Emily." He paused then opened his mouth but turned his head quickly and began coughing.

She watched, concern swirling her stomach. "You're still sick. You need to be in bed, not working in the barn."

He turned back. "I'll be fine." Sweat beaded his brow again.

She bit her lip, nodded.

He took a step closer, and she thought she could feel his warmth in the cool night air. "Try to forget about all of that and get a good night's sleep." His voice was barely above a whisper. "Promise?" He reached up and ran a knuckle down her cheek.

She hoped he couldn't see her heart beating in her throat. She swallowed. "I promise."

He dropped his hand and gave her a lazy grin. "Good." He bent over and retrieved her packages and handed them to her.

She smiled back as she took them. "Good night, Josh. I'll be praying for you. And thank you again."

"Good night, Emily."

She turned and left the barn on shaky legs. But she hadn't crossed the yard when she heard Josh's cough start up again.

ENSCONCED IN BED, Emily slit open Mrs. Luke's letter but didn't unfold it. She didn't think she'd be able to keep her promise to Josh to forget everything and get a good night's sleep. Feelings stirred in her, and she didn't know how to make sense of any of it. She didn't want to think of Josh as a replacement for Thomas. They were very different men. But perhaps Josh was more like her.

Thomas was a friend, a good one, but Josh felt like maybe he could be much more. But if he ever knew everything about her past and rejected her, it would break her heart. There would no future based on lies—ironically Silas had taught her that—but maybe, once the money had been returned, she could tell him. Everything. Not just the pieces he knew now.

His cough concerned her. He'd been sick since he came back with the mules but seemed to be better. Now the cough was back, and he felt as if he were burning up with fever. Her own face warmed at the memory of how she knew how hot he was.

She hoped for his sake that he'd be well enough to finish fixing the cottage roof tomorrow. She had high hopes that she'd be nestled in her own cozy place by the time school started. But if Josh was sick, that wouldn't happen. But more importantly, it would mean that Josh was too sick to work and that would concern her greatly.

The verse about casting her cares on the Lord came to mind, and she crawled out of bed to find her Bible. After flipping through the pages, she found it. First Peter 5:7: "Casting all your care upon him; for he careth for you."

He did care for her, as hard as it was for her to believe it at times. She had to trust Him with her future. And with Josh's health.

Wasn't that always what Mrs. Luke was telling her? She flipped open the letter, reading the words of encouragement from her oldest and dearest friend. It was as if Mrs. Luke always knew just what she needed to hear. This time was no different. She asked how Emily found things in Reedsville and if her plans were falling into place. But also encouraged her to trust God with the mystery of life and to look to Him for guidance and direction. With those words wrapping her like a warm quilt, she blew out the lamp and snuggled down, prayers for Josh and for guidance the last thing on her mind before sleep took her.

JOSH PUT a warmed brick in his bed. He was cold and couldn't get warm. Whatever he had caught on his trip to the Joneses' was back. He wanted to finish the cottage for Emily, to replace that oilcloth with real shingles, but as bad as he felt, he didn't dare climb a ladder. Still, he hated to disappoint her.

As he got ready for bed, he thought about how much he had enjoyed talking with her, learning more about her. He was surprised Silas wasn't her blood grandfather. Although, he himself was as loyal to Maggie and Josiah Blake as if they were blood, so he could understand her loyalty and devotion to Silas.

They'd both had less-than-idyllic childhoods. Having a common bond with her made him want to strengthen their connection. Something he never would have expected when he picked her up at the Oregon Express office. What had been her real feelings for Thomas?

More than anything, he wanted to keep her safe. He was glad Mike Riley was on it, but seeing that man grab her today made his heart stop. His feelings were stronger than just enjoying having something in common. And he wasn't sure what to do about that.

The look on her face when he'd given her the gifts had made him glad he'd done it. Was it too much too soon? He didn't know, but she'd clearly enjoyed them, and he'd done something special for her, something no one else had ever done. A piece of his chest cracked a bit at the thought.

He climbed under the covers and tucked his feet close to the brick. He still shivered.

As he said his prayers, he added one for Emily. Just before he drifted off, he prayed for Pa, realizing he hadn't heard from him since that last letter. Should he be concerned? He fell asleep before he could wrestle that issue.

EMILY LOOKED out the back door for what must have been the hundredth time that day. She hadn't seen Josh since he'd come over this morning for a late breakfast. He was so pale, and his cheeks were bright red. Maggie gave him a cup of her willow bark tea then sent him back to bed. The fact that he didn't protest told Emily how sick he really was.

But this time she saw Seth and Becca pulling up. Her heart lifted. She was looking forward to this visit.

The smell of the broth bubbling on the stove made her stomach rumble. Maggie had started it just after breakfast, thinking it would cure what ailed Josh. But he hadn't shown up for it yet.

Becca and Seth entered, shaking off the rain. After hugs all around, Maggie shooed everyone into the dining room. A soup kettle and a basket of sourdough rolls sat on the table. And Emily knew there were apple turnovers for dessert.

After Seth said the blessing, Emily realized Josh really wasn't coming for supper. She hoped he was resting.

Becca stirred her soup around and stifled a yawn.

Maggie's brow furrowed. "You're not sick, too, are you?"

Becca waved her hand. "No, I just got over it. But I am tired. It's all this rain. What do you mean 'too'?"

"Josh is sick. That cough of his is back. And I've never seen him look so pale." Maggie passed the rolls around the table again.

After the turnovers and coffee had been served, Maggie insisted that Becca and Emily visit in the parlor.

Emily started to protest and decided against it. It didn't pay to argue with Maggie.

In the parlor, Becca and Emily shared the settee. The fire was comforting.

"How are *you* doing, Emily, after what happened?" Becca took a sip of coffee.

"I try not to dwell on it."

Becca looked at her expectantly.

"It was such an ordinary thing, walking out to the corral. And then he was grabbing me. Right in the yard." She shook her head. "It just doesn't seem possible that that could happen."

Becca nodded, eyes sympathetic. "Did you know I was attacked last spring?"

A jolt shocked Emily's chest. Becca? She seemed so perfect. Why would something bad happen to her? "How did it happen, if you don't mind my asking?"

"I was walking in the woods when two men grabbed me. Luckily—or I should thank God's protection—Seth had seen me go into the woods on his way to town. He kept an eye out for me and heard my screams. I only ended up with scrapes and bruises, but it could have been much worse. Seth and Josh caught the men and turned them over to the county sheriff.

Even though they had been caught, I didn't want to leave the house."

Emily was silent for a moment, deciding what to say. "There's always someone around, and that helps. Also, I don't think he wants me. He just wants the money." Her stomach soured. It was awful not sharing with Becca as honestly in return. Now it just wasn't Josh and Mike Riley she was lying to, but Becca who was trying to be her friend. No one had done that for her since Mrs. Luke.

Except for Josh. But it wasn't the same kind of friendship as with another woman.

Maggie joined them in the parlor, asking Becca about a quilting project.

Emily let her mind wander back to her Bible reading this morning in Psalm 46 about God being a refuge, "a very present help in trouble." This was a time of trouble for her. So why didn't God feel like her refuge? Maybe the answer was later in the psalm where it said to "be still and know that I am God." She puzzled over this verse, wondering why it came after descriptions of God's mighty works.

Perhaps that was the point. *God is mighty, so why am I trying to control something that should remain under His control?* But where did one draw the line? Where did she take action, do her duty to Silas, and where should she just let things happen as they may?

McKay walked into Blake's Dry Goods in Portland, the little bell above the door tinkling. The older man behind the counter looked in his direction and nodded before returning to his customer. McKay wandered around the aisles, appearing to look at the merchandise. He scanned the store out of the corner of his eye, noticing how it was laid out. If that woman had left the money here, where would it be hidden?

The man behind the counter—he was certain it was Blake—was still helping his customer. Though silver covered the man's hair, he was still trim and fit, his movements quick and sure. He wasn't someone they could cower with the threat of physical violence. They'd have to sneak in here and find the money themselves.

He looked out the front window to where Dillon stood across the street, leaning against the wall. Catching his eye, McKay nodded slowly. Dillon pushed away from the wall, crossed the street and disappeared from view.

He picked a few staples from the shelves and made his way toward the counter. Blake disappeared behind a velvet curtain—to the storeroom, McKay thought—then returned. The customer left, and Blake was addressing him. "Good afternoon. Will that be all?"

"I need a plug of tobacco as well."

Josiah nodded and went to fetch it. McKay leaned against the counter. A set of stairs began just past the storeroom, probably to Blake's apartment. They'd have to be careful tonight. He looked over his shoulder and out the window again. Dillon leaned against the wall.

Josiah returned, and McKay paid for his purchases and left the store.

The twins waited until dark before walking up the street to the Oregon Express office. A sign in the window said due to weather conditions it was closed until further notice. They walked past the office, but no one else was around. All the businesses on this street were closed for the night. McKay leaned against the porch column while Dillon went around back. A moment later, he heard a click behind him, and the door to the Oregon Express office stood ajar.

Glancing up the street one more time, he entered the office. He hoped the money was here; it would make things so much easier.

Dillon was already behind the counter rifling through papers.

"Hey, be careful. We don't want anyone to know we were here."

"Why? They ain't gonna know it was us."

McKay shook his head. He didn't know why he even tried to reason with Dillon. This was the absolute last time he got his brother out of trouble.

He looked around the rest of the office. There wasn't much here. A few chairs, a bench, and a stove in the main waiting area, and a desk behind the counter.

"Aha!" Dillon lifted a strongbox out of the desk drawer and shook it.

"It sounds empty."

"Greenbacks don't make no sound." He pulled a wire out of his pocket and stuck it in the lock, fiddling with it until the latch sprung open. It was empty.

"Told you."

Dillon's face darkened, and he heaved the box across the room. It hit the shelf of mugs above the stove, sending them crashing to the floor.

McKay rushed to the window and looked out. Seeing nothing, he spun around. "What are you doing? Are you out of your mind? Someone could have heard that, and they'll know for sure we were here. I'm risking my neck helping you out here."

In two strides Dillon was nose to nose with his brother. "Look here, McKay. You think you're all high and mighty, but you're in this just as deep as I am. If Dawson and his gang think I've lost that money, I'm a dead man. And they'll come after you next."

McKay heard the panic in his brother's voice. And it was there for good reason. Dawson wasn't known for his mercy. Anyone he thought had double-crossed him was dealt with ruthlessly, buried in unmarked graves as a warning to anyone who might think of betraying him.

The only reason McKay had agreed to help Dillon out was to save his neck. He just wished Dillon had the sense never to get involved with Dawson's gang in the first place.

Dillon stepped back, face pale and eyes wide. His hands shook before he stuffed them in his pockets.

McKay ran his hand over his face. "All right. It's not here. Let's go check out Blake's place.

Chapter Thirteen

Becca and Seth left to get home before it got dark. The rain made the visibility difficult enough. As Emily waved goodbye to them, she looked out past the barn toward Josh's cabin. Here it was almost dark, and he'd missed supper. She drummed her fingers on the doorjamb.

"Maggie, do you think we should check on Josh and bring him something to eat?"

"I was just thinking that myself. Why don't you put together a basket?"

"I was thinking some of the stew, a few biscuits, more of your willow bark tea, and a few things so he won't have to leave the cabin if he doesn't care to..." Her voice trailed off as she reached for a basket. In no time at all she had it stuffed with items for Josh. She set it by the back door. "Maggie, are you ready?"

She turned around just in time to see a glass slip from Maggie's hand and bounce on the floor. Emily froze, unable to help as Maggie grabbed for the glass but missed. It slammed into the stove and shattered.

"Ouch!" Maggie jerked her hand back. Blood oozed from her finger and started to drip on the floor.

"Oh, here." Emily snatched up the dishcloth and pressed it to Maggie's finger. Glass crunched under her feet. "Keep that on your finger, and I'll sweep up the glass."

Maggie replaced Emily's hand with her own. "No, you go on over to Josh's. With the rain, it'll be too dangerous to cross the footbridge once it's dark, which will happen before I can get this cleaned up."

Emily backed toward the door, careful of the glass on the floor. "Are you sure?" She glanced out the kitchen window. "We might still have a few minutes of light left."

"No, if you don't go now, you won't get back across before dark."

Emily bent down and picked up the basket. "If you're sure, I'll just drop this off and be right back."

Maggie pulled the rag back and looked at her cut. "Yes, dear. I'll see you in a few minutes."

Emily wrapped herself in her shawl, opened the kitchen door, and hurried down the porch steps. Clouds obscured a quickly darkening sky. Only a light mist fell, but the ground was sodden as Emily made her way to the footbridge that led to Josh's cabin. It took her a minute to realize what she was seeing.

The creek lapped at the bottom of the elevated bridge. It had overflowed its banks for days, but she'd never seen it this high.

She approached it, gaze darting back and forth, and thought about turning back. But as sick as Josh was, most likely he couldn't get across the bridge. If she didn't bring him food now, he might have nothing until morning. She had no idea what supplies he kept in his cabin. Tomorrow she was certain Maggie would insist Josh come stay at the boardinghouse until he was well. Seth could help him after church, if need be.

With the basket balanced over her arm, she grabbed her skirt with both hands. She took a large step over the water and splashed onto the cut log that served as the bottom step. Stepping on to the second log, she studied the footbridge. Where the boards dipped in the center, water flowed over the bridge.

She stepped on the boards slick with mud. Taking her time, she took one step after another. She couldn't help but see the creek was full of mud, tree branches, and brush, some of which wedged under the bridge. Fear swirled through her stomach as she stepped in the water covering the middle of the bridge. She put her foot out, testing the boards before trusting them with her full weight. They gave slightly but seemed to hold. She quickened her steps across the rest of the bridge, hopped down the stairs, and over to Josh's cabin.

Once under the shelter of his porch, she let out her breath. She rapped on the door, then stepped back to look around. She hadn't been here before.

His cabin was built solidly out of logs that had been hewn flat on the tops and bottoms to join snugly. And unlike most, it had a front porch and glass windows. It did not look tall enough to be two stories, yet she had seen dormer windows above the porch.

She knocked again. "Josh? It's Emily." The gray twilight was rapidly darkening, and she dreaded crossing that bridge again. Every moment she waited made the crossing more dangerous. "Josh?" Tension built in her chest. Setting the basket down, she paced to the nearest window and peered in.

It was the room the front door opened into. Directly opposite the door was a massive stone fireplace with logs stacked on one side and a thick braided rag rug in front. The furniture was large and sparse. It had a masculine air but was well-kept.

There was no sign of Josh. She craned her neck. There was a doorway to the right she supposed led to the kitchen. She moved to the edge of the window to get a better angle. And then she saw it.

A booted foot sticking out of the doorway.

EMILY THOUGHT her heart would beat right out of her chest. There was no telling how long Josh had been lying there.

She hurried to the front door. It was highly improper, but she didn't care. Josh could have hit his head and be bleeding to death. Everyone at the boardinghouse would understand, and no one else would need to know.

The front door moved easily on well-oiled hinges as Emily pushed it open. She picked up the basket, stepped through the doorway, and shut the door behind her. Taking a deep breath, she crossed the room to the kitchen.

Josh lay on the floor, a cup shattered next to him.

She set the basket on the kitchen table and knelt next to him. She didn't see any blood. That was a relief. "Josh, can you hear me?" He didn't move. She picked up his hand and rubbed it. It was so much bigger and heavier than hers, the calluses rough against her palm. His hand was hot. She dropped it and reached to his forehead. He was burning up.

Taking him by the shoulders she shook him. "Josh, wake up." She used her sternest schoolmarm voice.

His head moved. "Emily?" His words were slurred, and he didn't open his eyes.

"Yes, it's me. Can you get up? You need to be in bed." She pulled on his arm, getting his shoulders off the floor.

"Tired."

"I know. You can rest once you're in bed." She put her other hand behind his shoulder, trying to push him up. But without his help, she couldn't get him to his feet. "Come on, Josh. I need your help. You have to stand up."

He was sitting now. He looked at her, his eyes glassy, as if noticing her for the first time. "Why are you here?"

"You're sick. Now stand up so we can get you to bed."

He bent his knees. She moved next to him, putting his arm around her shoulder and hers around his waist. With great effort, he got to his feet, Emily taking on much of his weight. She nudged him forward, turning slightly so they could get through the doorway. They stumbled across the main room to the bedroom on the other side.

Josh mumbled something, but she didn't have any spare energy to ask him to repeat himself. Dragging him into his bedroom, she tried to lower him onto his bed, but his weight was too much for her and he flopped down.

For a moment she stood there, trying to catch her breath, wishing her corset was looser. She bent down and lifted his legs on the bed. He seemed to be asleep again. He would have to sleep in his clothes, but his boots needed to come off. Bracing herself against the foot of the bed, she grasped a boot and tugged until it came off, nearly sending her sprawling. She repeated the process with the second one then set them at the foot of the bed.

As she tucked a quilt around him, he reached for her face. "So pretty," he mumbled.

Her cheeks burned. But her heart swelled. Yes, he was delusional, but he did think her pretty. She pushed the thought aside. If he was awake at all, she should try and get some broth into him. No telling when he had last had something to eat.

She got some broth in a bowl and prodded him to sit up enough. She spooned a bit into his mouth. He took a few swallows before sliding down under the covers. It would have to do.

She wet a cloth in the kitchen and laid it across his burning forehead. Hoping he would sleep well through the night, she wrapped her shawl around her shoulders and stepped outside. Seth would have to carry Josh back to the boardinghouse tomorrow. He couldn't stay here alone when he was so sick. But for tonight, there was nothing to be done.

It was pitch black outside, the clouds and rain blotting out any light. She watched her step, wishing she'd brought a lantern. She had no desire to end up in the raging creek. She could hear where it was, and the closer she got, the more she looked for the footbridge. Finally, she spotted the steps.

But the rest of the bridge was no longer visible, debris washing over it as if it weren't there.

McKay paced the alley while Dillon fiddled with the back doorknob of Blake's Dry Goods. "Hurry up! Before someone sees us."

"Done." Dillon pushed the door open. "Never worry, brother. I know what I'm doing."

"Then why are *we* in this mess?" McKay whispered as he edged past Dillon into the storeroom. "Never mind. Just look for the money, and let's get out of here."

McKay's heart pounded as he quietly moved boxes and sacks around looking for hidden money. The sound of something hitting the floor in the store froze McKay. Why couldn't Dillon be more careful? McKay edged quietly toward the front.

Dillon was edging a knife blade around the cash register drawer.

The squeak of a floorboard came from overhead.

McKay poked Dillon's shoulder. "Now you've woken him up. Let's go." He spun and headed toward the storeroom. Dillon wasn't behind him.

Another squeak. This one sounded like it came from the stairs.

McKay swore under his breath. Dillon! Leaving the back door open, McKay edged into the storeroom, looking for Dillon. Why wasn't he coming?

A large crash from the bottom of the stairs sent McKay flying the rest of the way in.

Josiah Blake lay crumpled at the bottom of the stairs.

Dillon held a broomstick and then dropped it. He ran past McKay. "Let's go before he wakes up!"

"Dillon! Why did you do that?" McKay was torn between helping Josiah and getting caught. He knelt by the older man. No blood, and he was stirring. "I'm sorry. I really am." McKay stood and spun, heading out the door after Dillon.

FROZEN, Emily barely noticed she was getting soaked by the rain. What should she do? There was no good solution. Her reputation would be ruined if anyone discovered she had spent the night in Josh's cabin, regardless of how sick he was. And her hopes for becoming a respectable townsperson, let alone the schoolmarm, would be in tatters.

Yet, risking crossing the footbridge, if it was even still there, was to risk death. Death or death of her reputation? The choices seemed nearly equal.

She hurried back to the cabin and found a lantern. She lit it and made her way back out to the raging creek. With the lantern, she still couldn't see the footbridge.

Another light bobbed across the way. And the someone shouted her name. Maggie!

"I'm over here! But the bridge isn't crossable!" Emily held the lantern up near her face.

The lantern across the way shifted and sent a glow over two people. Maggie and James. "Stay there. Don't try to cross. It's too dangerous." A pause. "How is Josh?"

"Very sick. I found him unconscious in the kitchen. I got a bit of broth in him, but he's burning up with fever." She shivered at the memory of finding him on the floor, wondering for a brief moment if he was dead.

"It's good you're with him then. Someone needs to tend to him."

Emily nodded then realized Maggie probably couldn't see her head. "Yes. We'll see how things are in the morning."

"Be careful. You'll be in my prayers." Then the lantern across the way bobbed towards the boardinghouse and was swallowed in darkness.

Leaving her with nothing but the encompassing darkness and the sound of the raging creek.

.

Chapter Fourteen

J osh's head pounded, and his eyes burned. His mouth felt like he'd been eating sawdust. Faint light came through the windows, but he had no idea what time it was.

Carefully he moved his head. What? He rubbed his eyes. Surely he was seeing things. What was Emily doing sitting in a chair by the fireplace reading? He was hallucinating. That was it. His heart squeezed. The image seemed so right. Like a wish he hadn't known he'd made. He closed his eyes to hang on to the vision.

He heard a rustling and opened them.

Emily made her way toward him. "Are you awake?" Her voice was soft. Her cool hand landed on his forehead.

"Why are you here?" His voice was scratchy and dry.

"I found you lying on the kitchen floor last night when I came to bring you some food. You were burning up. You're still warm, but maybe a little cooler. Would you like some broth?"

He nodded and closed his eyes. He heard noises from the kitchen, and a minute later she was saying, "See if you can sit up."

He pushed himself to a sitting position and took the bowl she offered. His hand shook, but he managed to get the spoon to his mouth. The broth felt warm and wonderful sliding down his sore throat. He got through nearly half the bowl before exhaustion overtook him.

"Here, I'll get that." She took the bowl from him. "Rest and you can have more later."

He nodded as he slid back under the covers.

As her hands tucked the quilt under his chin, it occurred to him that if she had found him last night, then she must have spent the night here. That could create some problems, but he was too tired to think of what they might be. Sleep claimed him.

EMILY LOOKED INTO THE BEDROOM. Josh stirred in his sleep a few times, but he seemed to rest easier than he had during the night. She had slept in the chair flanking the fire so she could listen for him.

This morning, she made coffee and ate some of the biscuits and scrambled up some eggs Maggie had sent over. She cleaned the kitchen and wandered around the cabin, waiting for him to wake. It was still gray and rainy. She didn't have to go outside to see that the footbridge was still underwater. The vestiges of guilt clung to her that he'd gotten sick fixing her cottage. He had seemed like he was getting better, but maybe if he'd rested instead of working... There was really no way to know, but the guilt remained.

There was a set of steep stairs leading to an additional sleeping loft, which explained the dormers on the front of the cabin. She climbed them to find two beds and a couple of crates. This must have been where Thomas and Seth had slept when they had all lived together. No personal items remained, not that she expected them to, but it was comforting to see what had once been Thomas's personal space. Only fondness surfaced, as for an old friend, when she thought of him now.

Downstairs, she found a lovely carved bookcase. Josh's work, obviously. She ran her hand over the silky wood, imagining him working on it by firelight some cold, winter night. There was a collection of books, including some of Mr. Twain's, *Innocents Abroad* and *Tom Sawyer*. She smiled. She hadn't picked Josh as a reader, yet these books seemed exactly like what he would read. And it explained his ability to discuss Mr. Twain with her.

She had tucked *Roughing It* in the basket she had brought. Even though she was only half way through it, she thought he might enjoy borrowing it while he was convalescing. It was about Mr. Twain's adventures out West, including some involving a stagecoach, which she thought Josh would find particularly entertaining.

Shivering, she moved to stir the fire and add more wood, then refilled her coffee mug. She pulled the book from the basket and set it on a side table, moving a letter that lay open. She couldn't help but see that it was from Josh's father.

Her eyes were drawn back to the letter. Wouldn't his father want to know that Josh was sick? Josh hadn't been overly forthcoming on the subject, but he had said his pa had been prone to drink.

As tempted as she was to read the letter, she flipped it face down. She wouldn't want Josh to read her private correspondence to Silas. A shudder went through her at the thought. But maybe the letter meant that there was restoration with his pa. She hoped there was.

She needed to occupy her mind, so she opened *Roughing It*. As long as Josh was asleep, there was nothing for her to do. And if she had her own thoughts to keep her company... Well, that just wouldn't do.

Because all she could think about was how school was to start tomorrow. She had to get over that bridge by then and keep the news of her presence here from going beyond the boardinghouse.

Josh opened his eyes. Emily was still reading. Was he still imagining her? His stomach growled, and he was hungry. He wasn't dreaming.

He pushed himself up.

She looked over and smiled.

He could get used to seeing that smile when he woke up. He didn't even try to push the thought away. He was sick. Who knew what directions his thoughts would wander?

"How are you feeling?"

"Hungry."

She hurried over and touched his forehead again. "No fever. And being hungry is a good sign. I'll bring you some broth." She disappeared into the kitchen, but he wished he could have kept her hand on his head. Her touch was so soft.

She brought him a bowl of broth.

He had gotten several spoonfuls in before he slowed down. She was still watching him, and he felt a bit sheepish. He nodded toward the book she had set on the foot of his bed. "What are you reading?"

She picked up the book and smiled. "Your gift, *Roughing It*. There are a few stagecoach stories in here I think you'll find amusing. I see you have *Innocents Abroad*. Have you read it?" She tilted her head toward the bookcase.

"Some. I like his sense of humor, and he's good at telling a story. But I'm not much of a reader. I mostly read the Bible. Short segments that I can mull over while I'm taking care of the horses or driving the stage." He went back to his soup. Telling a schoolmarm he didn't like to read seemed like a good way to doom their friendship.

"I've found students who don't catch on to reading right away or aren't taught properly can have difficulty attaining enough performance to enjoy reading." She opened the book. "How about I read while you eat?"

She settled on the foot of his bed and began to read while he finished his soup. He emptied the bowl and wanted to ask if there was more, but he loved hearing her voice. She made the story come alive in a way it never did when he tried to read.

She noticed his bowl was empty and closed the book. "I have some of Maggie's biscuits. Does that sound good?"

"It does, but will you keep reading while I eat?" He didn't want her to stop.

She graced him with one of her room-brightening smiles. "Of course."

After he finished two of Maggie's biscuits and a cup of coffee, he needed to use the privy. He was still in his clothes, he was glad to see, and his boots rested on the floor near his bed. He reached for them and pulled them on.

Emily stopped reading and raised her eyebrows. "Going somewhere?"

"I'll be back." But he didn't look at her, hoping she wouldn't ask any more questions.

"Ah. Okay."

He felt weak as a kitten when he stood, but he needed to get out of bed. He steadied himself, knowing her eyes were on him. He headed out the back of the cabin and made a quick trip to the privy. The fresh air was bracing but refreshing. It was drizzling, and the sky was black to the west. A few flashes of lightning lit up the dark clouds far away. He glanced over the creek. It had completely buried the footbridge, explaining why Emily couldn't leave. He could only imagine what it had been like crossing it on her way here. She was a brave woman, he would give her that.

Brave in more ways than one. If word got out that she had stayed here, her reputation would be ruined.

Unless he married her. The thought slammed into him with such force he grabbed the side of the cabin. Would she even want to be married to an uneducated man?

He shook his head. Better cross that bridge when he came to it. If he came to it.

EMILY CLEANED up the dishes and tidied the kitchen while Josh was outside. She took the Twain book and moved it to the living room. She enjoyed reading to him. There was a quiet coziness to their situation, one she rather liked, as long as she didn't think about what tomorrow might bring. She had to be at the schoolhouse in the morning or her life was ruined.

The back door opened, and Josh entered, shaking the damp off him. She hurried over to give him a kitchen towel. "Don't relapse just as you're getting better."

He took the towel and grinned. "It'll take more than a little rain. I'm definitely on the mend." He rubbed his head with the towel, making his curls stand up.

"More coffee?"

"Sure." He took a chair from next to the fireplace and moved it to face the window. He did the same with the second chair.

She brought over two mugs and raised her eyebrows.

"There's a storm coming, and I like to watch them."

She almost dropped the mugs. Trembling shook her from head to toe. Where could she hide? Could she shove one of Josh's pillows over her head?

He took his mug and then her hand. "It will be fine. We're inside. It can't hurt us."

She allowed herself to be led to the chair and sat stiffly.

"Tell me more about your life with Silas. Did you always live in Portland?" Josh sat in the other chair, sipping from his mug. Other than being a bit pale, she would have never known he had been so sick.

"How can you sit there so relaxed? Aren't you worried about what people might be thinking? About the animals? And your chores?"

"There's nothing I can do about any of it. Maggie is wise and won't say anything. James knows how to take care of the animals when I'm not there. Pastor Adams, if he even knows you're here, strikes me as a man who values compassion over propriety. I can't even worry about when the Oregon Express might run again or what could happen if it doesn't. I don't like that idea at all, but only God can control any of that." He sat back and sipped his coffee. "When I work, I work hard, and I focus on doing a good job. But I learned early on that there is much of my life I have no control over."

Her heart softened. She could only imagine how scared he must have been as a boy with a sick ma and a pa who wasn't reliable.

A flash of lightning. She jumped and then stilled, waiting for the roar of thunder.

He reached over and took her hand. "It's okay."

She licked her lips and took a breath. This was a silly fear. He was right. She was safe here.

He squeezed her hand. "Tell me about your life with Silas. Was it good?"

Security flowed from his hand into hers. She met his gaze and saw understanding and openness there. She swallowed. "Silas was a huckster. We moved from town to town while he ran his schemes. He would dress me up and people wouldn't suspect a thing until he had cheated them out of everything or picked their pockets. Most of the time we left town before the people figured it out, but a few times we had to sneak out in the middle of the night."

Another flash and this time the crash of thunder followed more quickly. The storm was getting closer. She squeezed Josh's hand and closed her eyes.

"How did you get from that lifestyle to working at the Hotel Portland?"

His question had only interest, no judgment. The tension in her chest began to slightly loosen. "One day I heard singing and stopped to listen. It was a tent revival meeting. I stood in the back and heard a man talk about Jesus. About how much He loved me and died so all my sins would be washed away. I wanted that. More than anything. I came back night after night, not telling Silas."

She stared out the window, remembering. "One night, the pastor's wife, Mrs. Luke, came up to me. She was so kind. She invited me to her house the next day for cookies and lemonade. She led me in a prayer of salvation. She told me Jesus would cleanse me and make me a new creature." She sighed. "Even though I was a new creature, people still saw me as the old creature. Eventually, when I was old enough, I went to Portland to lose myself in the big city and start over. Mrs. Hanson gave me a job, and I studied and studied until I could pass the teacher's examination."

She finally met Josh's gaze. The compassion she found there had her blinking away tears.

Thunder crashed above the house, and she jumped, yanking her hand from his, and curling into a ball in the chair.

"Emily."

She peeked above her arms.

Josh stood in front of her. "Come here." He took both of her hands and tugged her out of the chair. He pulled her in front of him and turned her to face the window. Standing behind her, he wrapped his arms around hers over her middle. Her head tucked under his chin.

The lightning flashed again, and she tensed.

Josh pulled her tight. "It's going to be okay. I've got you. You're safe."

His broad chest cradled her safely. She became more aware of his heat bleeding through her blouse, his thick arms holding her close. His breath moved the loose hair across the top of her head. She was so aware of his presence that the thunder crashed around her, but she didn't tense. Her focus was completely on Josh.

She barely breathed through the next round of thunder and lightning. But she didn't tense up. She could do this. With Josh's help, she was surviving a thunderstorm.

She turned in his arms to thank him, only to come face to face with his intense gaze, eyes like melted chocolate. "Josh, I—"

His head dipped, and his gaze lowered briefly before meeting hers again. She stepped deeper into his arms. His head lowered, and his lips touched hers. Lightly at first, and then deeper, more possessive. She kissed him back, pouring all of the relief and fear and joy into her kiss.

When the kiss broke, her arms were around his neck.

Suddenly, the reality of their situation hit her. They could not be doing this. She pushed out of his arms.

Chapter Fifteen

Josh opened his eyes. His head didn't hurt. He threw off the covers, still in his clothes. He'd felt stronger, but he was on the mend. Light slanted across the living room floor. Both of the chairs were back by the fireplace. Emily wasn't in either of them. He padded out to the kitchen. The stove was warm, the coffee pot full, but no Emily.

Maybe she'd gone out to the privy? He pulled his boots on and went outside. The ends of the footbridge were visible now. The creek had receded a bit, but water still flowed over the middle of the bridge. Muddy footprints on the far side of the bridge told him one thing: Emily was gone.

He couldn't believe she'd risked going over that footbridge. If she had slipped… He couldn't even imagine.

On the other hand, if she hadn't opened the school on time this morning, there would be too many questions. Ones neither one of them wanted to answer. But the brunt would fall most heavily on Emily. She would lose her teaching position. Then what would she do?

If it were up to him, he'd want her to stay in Reedsville. And he hoped her kindness in caring for him didn't put that in jeopardy.

As THE LAST child left the schoolroom, Emily let out the breath that had been trapped in her lungs all day. She'd done it! A successful first day back at school. For the most part, things went smoothly. Most of the children had been her students before and were happy to see her.

She packed up her books and then wiped down the chalkboard. She had a glimmer of hope that she could become a respectable member of this town. Even without Thomas.

The schoolhouse door opened, and she turned.

Josh stood in the doorway, grin on his face.

"Josh!" She grabbed her things and headed toward him, worry and happiness competed for prominence in her heart. "What are you doing here? Should you be out of bed?" She reached to touch his forehead and then snatched her hand back.

"I'm fine. Just a little weak. Came to see how your first day went." His deep brown gaze met hers. "And to make sure you were safe after going across that footbridge. I can't believe you risked that."

They moved outside, and she locked the door behind them. Scanning the area to ensure they were alone, she headed down the stairs. He reached for her books, and she let him take them. "I didn't have a choice, Josh," she said, softly. "You know that."

"I would have helped you. Given you a rope or something. I thought my heart would stop this morning when I saw what you had done."

She gave him a soft smile, and they headed toward the boardinghouse. "Thank you. But you needed to rest."

He waved her off. "I want to finish the cottage roof, probably not today, but I don't know that it's safe for you to stay there after that man grabbed you. Even if he doesn't believe you have the money, he could come back for revenge. We just don't know who we're dealing with."

She nodded. He was right. She didn't like it, but he was right. Until the money was back to its rightful owner, she had to be careful. For more reasons than one.

She was touched that Josh was concerned and had come to the schoolhouse. "Did you come to walk me home to keep me safe?"

He shrugged. "I wanted to make sure you were okay after this morning and, yeah, until that guy is caught, I don't think you should be going anyplace by yourself."

She started to bristle, but then thought back to how well he'd taken care of her last night through the thunderstorm. And then the kiss. Her face heated, and she stared at the road in front of her.

"I'm sure you're right."

Josh started coughing.

"Don't tell me you're surprised that I agreed." She smiled at him, covering her concern that his cough was back.

He gave her a wry smile.

"You overdid it coming to get me."

"If James doesn't walk you and Sally to school each day, I will."

Her heart warmed. She touched his arm. "Thank you. No one has cared about me like this since Mrs. Luke."

"The pastor's wife you were telling me about last night. Tell me more about her. You can talk the rest of the walk home, and I can save my breath."

She smiled. And her words took her back to another time.

WHEN MRS. LUKE invited her in for lemonade and cookies and treated her like a real lady, Emily thought she had died and gone to heaven.

Every time she had spotted women having tea in the hotel

dining room through the window she stopped and watched. They looked so elegant with their hats and the china and the dainty sandwiches and cookies. They laughed and seemed to be having a wonderful time. The waiters treated them with respect.

Her favorite thing was to play "tea" with whatever she could use as her guests: a box, an old stuffed sack, a discarded doll with a cracked head, a bear missing an arm. All things she had scavenged from the trash. Her most prized possession was a china tea cup with just a small chip in it that someone had thrown out.

So getting to have tea with Mrs. Luke was the happiest Emily had ever been. She daintily sipped her tea like she'd seen the ladies do in the hotel, using her best manners. She studied Mrs. Luke and copied her.

Mrs. Luke kept Emily's glass full and her plate piled with cookies. They discussed books and flowers and everything pleasant. Emily hoped they would have tea again.

It was short lived, however. Emily had tried to convince Silas that his schemes were wrong. When Silas wouldn't help her, she went to each person she could identify, told them about receiving Jesus, and tried to make things right. She took in nearly the whole town's wash to make up for what they had stolen.

Yet Emily nearly ended up in jail, and the townspeople had turned against Mrs. Luke for befriending Emily. She and Silas left town.

But Mrs. Luke had never stopped being Emily's friend, and she said Jesus wouldn't either. Wherever Emily went, Mrs. Luke wrote to her and encouraged her. Before Emily came to Reedsville, Mrs. Luke had been her only friend.

JOSH STEERED them toward the edge of the woods and a downed log. Emily might think he needed a rest, but in truth he didn't want to get back to the boardinghouse right away. Her words pierced his heart. A poor child being taken advantage of by adults, even when she was trying to do the right thing.

Once they were settled on the log, he took her hand. "I know a little how that feels. To do the right thing and still have people turn against you. I had been filling work orders my pa had gotten but was too drunk to finish. They started drying up as people knew Pa was a drunk. But when they found out I was filling the orders, they would sometimes give me the job, as long as I promised to keep away from Pa and his drunkenness. I won approval by working hard and taking care of Ma."

He gave a soft chuckle. "I don't usually talk about it. But I wanted you to know I understand."

Her gaze met his with softness. They had something in common, and he liked having her close. But should he let her? She took care of him at great risk to herself and her reputation.

"Josh, I—"

The sound of pounding footsteps them caught their attention. James was running toward them.

"Josh! Ben just delivered a telegram. The Oregon Express office in Portland was broken into."

EMILY HURRIED UPSTAIRS and put her school things away. She caught a glimpse of herself in the mirror over the washstand. She was still lying to Josh, to everybody, going on appearances. At least Josh had gotten a peek into who she really was. And he hadn't sent her packing. But she'd told so many lies she wasn't sure who she was anymore.

What would it be like to figure that out? Could she really admit to her fears, flaws, and inadequacies?

She sat on the bed, unable to look at herself anymore. She'd gone and fallen in love with Josh. And there was no way they could have any kind of future together if she didn't tell him everything.

He knew about her past.

If he could keep her secret about the thunderstorm and her staying at his cottage, could he keep her secret about the money? She had to find out.

Chapter Sixteen

With James walking Sally and Emily to and from school, it left Josh free to do a few light chores around the barn. As long as he didn't take a deep breath or work too hard, he didn't cough.

He'd taken the telegram about the Oregon Express office break-in to Mike Riley. They'd talked it back and forth, figuring there was a good chance it was related to the man who'd grabbed Emily looking for money. But since nothing seemed to be damaged or taken from his office, there wasn't anything to do.

As it got closer to the time for school to get out, he found reasons to look down the road.

But all he saw was Beth Paige, the town gossip, coming to visit Maggie. He ducked into the barn. Maggie could hold her own with Mrs. Paige, but Josh didn't want to get cornered about why he—and Emily—weren't in church Sunday. He hadn't talked to Maggie about it, so he didn't know what she had—or hadn't—told people. Pastor Adams was still making his rounds during the day and hadn't even given Josh or Emily so much as a sideways look at the supper table.

This was why he hated people nosing in his business. He and Emily would have to have a talk with Maggie and figure something out. Emily didn't need to be dragged through the mud for doing a kind thing. And other than their kiss, nothing improper had happened. Still, the rules of propriety weren't often logical.

He hid in the tack room and worked on repairing a harness.

He must have lost track of time because the barn door opened, and Emily stood there.

Her lip trembled, and her eyes welled.

"What's wrong?" He stood and pulled her into the tack room, guiding her to sit on the stool.

"Beth Paige knows. She came to confront Maggie about the licentiousness she allows under her roof. Maggie put her in her place, but she knew we were both missing from church on Sunday. I was well enough to teach, but everyone knows you were sick. Though Beth is implying that neither of us were sick, that we were using the empty boardinghouse as a trysting place."

"Well that's not true."

"You and I know that, but if Mr. Parsons or anyone else from the school board hears about it, I'll be fired. I couldn't wait for her to leave. As soon as she did, I came out here." Her voice broke and tears poured down her face.

He didn't know what to do. He'd never seen Emily cry, not at horses, not at thunderstorms. She was the bravest person he knew. He pulled out a handkerchief and handed it to her.

Kneeling in front of her, he took her hand in his. "Emily, it's going to be okay. I promise. Maggie will set everyone straight."

She nodded. "No one would dare think badly of Maggie."

They both smiled at that.

"May I ask you a question? About your ma?"

He wasn't expecting that. But after all that he had shared with her about his past, he couldn't think of anything he would keep from her. "Sure."

"How did you not become bitter at God? Because it feels like every time I try to do the right thing, I get punished."

He sighed and sat back on his heels. "Who says I wasn't? Let me tell you the story of what happened." He pulled over another stool and traveled back to the most painful period of his life.

MA LAY SHIVERING UNDER A BLANKET. Josh touched her forehead, and she was burning up. He shook the bottle next to the bed. All the medicine the doc had left was gone. And there wasn't money for more.

He'd scrambled around and done odd jobs for the shopkeepers, but there wasn't much work for a scrawny boy. Plus, he had to buy food.

Ma became delirious. Sorrow threatened to cut off his throat and stuffed his chest. He had to do something. But what? He couldn't leave her. But he had to help her. After trying to get her to drink a little tepid water, most of it ending up on the pillow, he knew he had to go find Pa.

Pulling his threadbare jacket around him, he took one last glance at Ma, asleep, though not necessarily peacefully.

He dashed through the cold, up and down the street at each bar until he spotted his dad, leaning over the counter, hand wrapped around an empty glass. He yanked on Pa's arm. "It's Ma. She's doing poorly. The medicine's all gone. You have to come help."

Pa shrugged off Josh. "I can't help her, boy. I can't even help myself."

"You have to. You have to try."

Pa shook his head and crumpled across the counter.

Josh yanked and pulled, hot tears filling his eyes, but Pa refused to budge. The jeers and comments of others barely touched his ears.

"Fine! Don't ever come back then. I don't need you." Josh ran out and back home. Bursting through the door, the silence covered him like a thick blanket.

Ma had gone, leaving the shell of her body behind. He threw

himself on her bed and wept, heart breaking. He'd never felt so alone. If he was only bigger, older, worked harder, Ma would still be alive.

EMILY'S HEART broke at the image of Josh as a boy losing his ma and his pa being no help. After hearing the whole story, she was glad she didn't meddle in his business and write to his father.

He took her hands in his. "I don't have an answer about why God allows bad things to happen to us. Especially when it seems it happens over and over. But I do know that He was always with me. And he gave me people like Maggie and Seth and Becca to walk with me on this journey of life. And for that I'm grateful."

She nodded. She wanted not only the peace that Josh had in God's goodness, but the deep friendships. Her mind flitted to Mrs. Luke, Mrs. Hanson, and now Maggie. God had provided.

"So do we need a plan? What do we say happened Sunday? Because Mr. Parsons is just looking for a reason to get rid of me and any hint of scandal—"

He rubbed his thumbs over her hands. "Least said, soonest mended. It'll blow over as soon as they have something else to talk about. Pastor Adams hasn't said anything, and if anyone would have a right to, it would be him."

"But what do I say? You were sick at your cabin, but I can't admit to being there. I don't want to lie." At least not anymore than she had been.

He met her gaze. "If anyone calls into question your reputation—" he swallowed—"we could get married."

She wasn't hearing him right. Surely he didn't just propose marriage? But before she could respond, he tugged her hands toward him and leaned forward, kissing her tenderly. He released one of her hands and cupped the back of her head. A kiss full of promise and a future. Everything she could want.

Except—

She pulled back. "I—we can't. I mean, I can't trap you in a marriage with me just out of your sense of honor." She squeezed his hand. "I'm grateful. Please know that's the kindest thing anyone has ever done for me." Tears spilled from her eyes and clogged her throat. "You should marry for love." Pulling her hand from his grasp, she fled the barn.

JOSH STARED out the door Emily had just disappeared through. He was at a loss as to what had just happened. Her words rang in his ears. *You should marry for love.* But he did love her. Guess he neglected to mention that. But he could finally put a name to those feelings that had been growing steadily since he saw her in Portland at the Oregon Express station.

Sure, he hadn't thought out the proposal. But he'd wanted to assure her that he would make everything okay, that he wouldn't abandon her or turn on her like the people in her past had.

Disappointment settled heavily on him. Surprising, since he hadn't thought about proposing in advance. But from the moment it entered his mind, it seemed so right. Now, he just had to convince her that he loved her and truly wanted to marry her beyond it being a convenience.

He pushed up from the stool. Working was better than thinking. James had done the bulk of the chores, but there was always something to do. He headed between the stalls to look in on the horses. His hands went to the routine without him thinking, allowing his thoughts to wander. He checked if the mangers had been cleaned and were full. There was one, unused stall. He stuck his head in it out of habit more than anything. But something didn't look right. What in the world? The manger hung on the wall crooked.

He bent down and looked around. Something was wedged in there, holding the manger away from the wall. Why would that happen? He reached up with his fingers and touched something soft. Too soft to be rotted wood. He tugged until he pulled it down and got a better grip. Finally, it came free.

A leather pouch. With a sinking feeling in his stomach, he opened it. But he knew what he would find.

Chapter Seventeen

J osh tied the final strap on the pack mules. The pearl gray sky was just beginning to show pink streaks in the east. He hated that he wasn't making the mail run, but both Maggie and Seth were right. He still wasn't strong enough, and if he relapsed, things would be much worse. Better to let Seth make this run and be well enough for the next one.

"Seth, I appreciate you taking this for me. Tell Becca I said thanks as well. She'll holler if she needs anything, right?"

"It's the least I can do. James will check in to help with anything Becca might need. Plus, the time away will just make her appreciate me more." He slapped Josh on the shoulder then mounted his horse.

At the mention of marriage, Josh's stomach turned. He hadn't talked to Emily since she'd run out last night. She hadn't come down for supper. Why hadn't she trusted him enough to tell him about the money? The fact that she hadn't hurt him more than he would have imagined. His heart was hollow and empty, just like when Ma died and Pa wasn't around.

Seth led the string of mules out of the yard and down the street. Waving him off, Josh couldn't help but think his life had spun out of his control.

WHILE IT TOOK EFFORT, Emily kept her mind on the lessons and her students instead of her emotional turmoil. Josh's proposal touched her heart and part of it, a big part of it, longed to just tell him yes. Why was she hesitating? Her feelings for him were stronger than they ever had been for Thomas. Couldn't Josh just replace Thomas in her plan?

The thought made her shudder. No, because her feelings were so strong for him, she wouldn't let him marry her for less than true love. She couldn't do that to him.

"Miss Stanton?" At the voice of eight-year-old Flossie Drake, Emily looked up, reeling in her wandering thoughts.

"We're done with the reading."

The second-year students stood, books in front of them. They had each read a page aloud and had finished. Apparently. Emily hadn't heard a word.

"Yes, thank you." She checked the watch pinned to her blouse. "Gather your things. School is dismissed."

Slowly, Emily wiped down the boards and gathered her things. She had avoided Josh at supper last night, but she wouldn't be able to do that forever. She would miss his friendship too much. How could she reclaim their closeness?

She closed the door behind her and locked it. When she turned to go down the stairs, Josh stood at the bottom. "Um, where are James and Sally?"

"I sent them home. We need to talk." Josh's face was hard, more serious than he'd ever seen him.

"What's wrong?" Her heart stopped. Had something happened to Maggie? Had the rumors about her and Josh spread even further?

He faced her. "I found the money. Tell me the truth, Emily. Don't lie to me. Tell me everything you know about it. Because I know you know more than you're telling."

Her mind reeled on instinct, thinking of a plausible story.

Stop. Not this time. She loved Josh, and if there was any hope of a future for them, she had to tell him the truth. He had to be the one person she could trust with everything. Even if it meant losing him.

Not being able to stand seeing the disappointment in his face, she returned to the schoolhouse steps and sat.

He sat next to her.

"I should have told you. I just— I'm not used to trusting anyone. I told you about what happened last time I tried to do the right thing. The idea of having to leave Reedsville and Maggie and Becca and—you—because I wasn't believed, well, it was just too painful to think about." She continued to tell him about finding the money in her valise, her assumption that Silas had stolen it, and her desire to let Silas have the opportunity to make it right. "When Seth gets back with the mail, I hope to have a letter from Silas." She turned to Josh. "I planned to talk to you as soon as I got that letter. I wanted to get your help and your advice. But mostly, I wanted you to know the truth."

His eyes were hooded; for the first time she could remember, she couldn't read his emotion. But at least he hadn't left.

"What about the man that grabbed you?"

"I told you the truth about that. I remembered him from the ferry. But I don't know what his connection is to the money. Is he the person Silas stole from? But how did he link it to me? I just don't know."

Dread washed over her. If the man knew Josh had it, would he be the next target? "Josh, where did you put the bank notes?"

"Don't worry. They're in the safe. Probably the most secure they've been the whole time you've had them." He held her gaze for a moment, gave a short nod then stood. He held out his hand. "Let's go home."

JOSH WALKED CLOSE ENOUGH to Emily on the way home that his arm brushed hers on occasion. As much as he was upset with her, he still liked having her close. And he was convinced she had told him the truth. He understood from her point of view why she didn't trust him. No one had believed her before. But somehow, he'd hoped she would have seen that he was different. While his heart was no longer hollow, it felt bruised and weak.

He didn't have any more words and neither did she. But the silence wasn't oppressive.

As the boardinghouse came into view, Emily touched his arm. "Could you wait to tell the sheriff until Seth gets back? I'd like to see if there's a letter from Silas. If there isn't, I'll go to the sheriff and tell him everything. But it's been this long, another few days won't matter."

He looked over, and her gaze melted his heart. He still wanted to do anything to make her happy.

He nodded.

Her smile warmed him clear through. He had done the right thing.

They entered the boardinghouse through the back door.

Sitting in Maggie's kitchen were two men, who came to their feet when they saw Emily.

"Emily, you remember Seth's pa, Josiah Blake."

"I do. Good to see you again."

Josh's gaze never left the second man. "And this is Charles Benson. My pa."

EMILY SPENT most of supper distracted and pretending she wasn't. She was comforted by Josh's response. In fact, her relief at his belief in her nearly weakened her knees on the walk home. It was more than she could have ever hoped for. She didn't dare dream that they would have any future together. That would be asking too much. She was simply grateful that he listened to her and didn't go straight to the sheriff.

Josh pushed his plate away. "So, what brings you gentlemen to our neck of the woods?"

Was she the only one that noticed the tight lines around Josh's eyes? His lighthearted words hid serious concern.

Josiah looked around the table. "I had a bit of trouble at the store. Someone broke in Saturday night. I heard noise down in the store and went to investigate. When I got to the bottom of the stairs, someone clobbered me. Gave me this." He pointed to the swollen bruise on the side of his head. "When I came to, they were gone and the back door was open. But other than rearranging a few things, nothing was taken. I must have interrupted them."

Josh's gaze met Josiah's. "That was the same night someone broke into the Oregon Express office. Same story there. Things rearranged but nothing taken." His gaze shifted to her.

She sat perfectly still, though she was squirming inside. She knew what he was thinking. This was all her fault. She had sent those men to Portland. They visited every place she had been, looking for the money. Which was in Josh's safe.

Her supper threatened to come up. She had no idea that those men would hurt anyone. What had she done?

What would Josh do? Would he blame her in front of everyone? Frankly, it would serve her right. She scrambled for some way to make this right. But there wasn't one.

His gaze on her softened.

Josiah continued. "Charlie stopped by the next morning. He told me about the Oregon Express break-in and came by to check on me. The two of us had a conversation and decided a trip out here might be warranted. Jake's watching the store, we borrowed some horses, and here we are. Maggie, I hope we can impose on your hospitality for a few days."

"You both are welcome to stay as long as you'd like. You're family. Now, how about some coffee and apple pie?"

Pastor Adams started to rise. "I'd be happy—"

Josh slid back his chair. "I'll help." His hooded gaze slid to Emily, and he shook his head. Okay, so he wanted to talk to Maggie alone. What was that about?

She caught Pastor Adams looking at the two of them. Her face heated. But he began sharing the local news he had gleaned from his visits.

Emily contributed by dredging up a few stories from school, all the while quaking inside at what Josiah had revealed and what Pastor Adams suspected.

And what Josh might do.

Josh helped Maggie grab plates and dish up pie. "Are you okay with them staying here? I'll talk to Pa and make sure he knows there's no drinking allowed here."

"They're more than welcome. I meant it when I said they were family. I'm glad Charlie came with Josiah. I wouldn't have wanted him to make that trip alone with that nasty bump on his head. And with Roy here, it's starting to feel downright homey."

Roy? Josh raised his eyebrows. Not that they were overly formal, but he'd never heard anyone refer to Pastor Adams by his Christian name. Though if anyone could get away with it, it'd be Maggie.

She slid the last piece of pie on a plate and met Josh's gaze. "But are you sure you don't want your pa staying with you? I don't mind him staying here at all, but it might be good for the two of you to spend some time together."

His shoulders tightened. "I suppose." He'd been avoiding Pa in Portland, and yet here he'd shown up on Maggie's doorstep. He couldn't avoid him any longer.

"It's going to be okay. Stop worrying. God hasn't stepped off His throne and left you in charge. This isn't like you, Josh."

He ran his hand over his face. "I know. I just can't seem to get a handle on things."

Maggie raised her eyebrows. "Or someone?" She touched his arm. "Every person in that dining room has been through a rough patch, you and me included. God has given us all a measure of grace. More than we deserve. We can spill some of it on others." She grabbed plates and headed to the dining room.

Josh grabbed the rest and followed.

Chapter Eighteen

J osh woke to the smell of bacon. It took him a minute to figure out why that was. Pa was here. And cooking.

He rubbed his face and got out of bed.

Over a breakfast of crisp bacon and surprisingly fluffy eggs, Josh considered what Pa would do all day. "I was pretty sick last week. Still not up to snuff. I could certainly use a pair of hands to help out if you're willing."

"That sounds like a good plan. I like to be useful, and I'd appreciate the chance." Pa took a sip of coffee. "I know I can't change the past, but I hope we could have a congenial future."

Josh nodded. He couldn't speak. Pa was trying, he had to give him that. How long he would try remained to be seen.

After breakfast and doing the chores in the barn, Josh had an idea. "Pa, you met Emily last night. She's the schoolmarm. The school board provided her with a cottage, and it needs its roof patched. Think you could help me with that today?"

Pa looked at the sky. "Seems a right nice day for it."

After getting a lunch pail from Maggie, they headed to the cottage.

Some of his tension slipped away as they worked companionably. "I think one more shingle ought to do it."

Pa handed it up to him. "That Emily seems like a nice girl. And right smart too, teaching school and all. A man could do worse."

Josh's eyebrows raised as he hammered in the shingle. Was Pa giving him courting advice? He scanned the roof in case he'd missed anything. Looked good. He climbed down the ladder. "I expect you're right."

"You know, I was looking around inside. Not much storage there. Wouldn't be too hard to build a cupboard for her."

"That's a great idea, Pa. We can look at the lumber scraps and see what we can do."

"I'm happy to do that since you've got so much to do. Find it's good to keep these old hands busy."

Josh nodded. He looked toward the school. Children streamed out. Must be lunch time. "Pa, you can start on lunch if you'd like. If you don't mind, I'd like to speak to the teacher."

"You go right ahead. I'm going to enjoy the sunshine while we have it."

A SHADOW PASSED over her desk. She hadn't even heard anyone come in. Emily looked up from the book she was reading. "Josh! I didn't expect to see you here."

"Pa and I repaired the roof on your cottage. It's ready, but until that man is caught, you should probably stay at Maggie's."

She nodded. He was right, and she had no desire to encounter that man again.

"I wanted to talk to you out of earshot of anyone, and with Josiah and Pa around, that's going to be harder. So that man believed you. He went to Portland and ransacked the Oregon Express office and Josiah's store, both places you had been. The only place he didn't go was the Hotel Portland. That we know of anyway."

"It wouldn't make sense for me to hide the money there.

There would be no way to ensure I could get into the room to retrieve it or that someone wouldn't stumble upon it before then. I could have entrusted it to Mrs. Hanson, but I don't think anyone from the outside would have known about our relationship. Given the places they went, it makes sense that they thought I hid the money somewhere and would be back for it. Which sounds just like something a criminal would do."

"The question is, since he didn't find the money, will he return? And if he does, I suspect he'll do more than just grab you."

She nodded. "Look at what happened to Josiah. I feel terrible about that. If I hadn't told the man to go to Portland…"

"You couldn't have known. But who knows how much worse it'll be next time. Please be careful and don't go anywhere alone."

She touched his arm. "Thank you for being concerned and for not telling everyone at the supper table that I was the cause of Josiah's pain."

"You're not the cause. That man was. Hopefully, Seth will bring good news tonight, and we can put this whole thing behind us."

She gave him a small smile. "I'd like that."

"I'd better get back and see if Pa left me any lunch."

"How is that going?"

He shifted his weight. "Better than I would have expected. But time will tell."

She glanced at her watch. Five minutes past the time she should have rung the bell. The one Josh had given her. The children wouldn't complain for sure, but she couldn't have word getting back to Mr. Parsons that she had a gentleman visitor during her lunch hour. "I'd better call the children in. Thanks for coming to see me. I'll see you and your father at Maggie's tonight?"

"Yep. I'll talk to James, make sure he knows to stick around you and Sally to and from school." He was almost out the door when she called his name.

He stopped and turned.

"Thank you. For everything."

He touched his hat and left.

AFTER SCHOOL, Emily deposited her things upstairs and then returned to the kitchen. She was pulling an apron over her dress when Pastor Adams entered the back door.

"Oh, hello. Done with your calls early?" She tied the strings around her waist.

"Yes. And the allure of Maggie's baking was too much for me to resist." He tossed his hat on the row of pegs as if he'd done it a thousand times.

"Oh, go on." Maggie waved a hand at him, but a soft pink colored her cheeks. Emily didn't think it was just from the stove. Maggie had a plate of cookies and a cup of coffee dosed with milk set on the table.

"Thank you, Maggie. Join me?" He pulled out a chair for her, and the pink in her cheeks intensified.

Emily pressed her lips together to hide a smile as Maggie sat. Should she leave? She felt a bit like an intruder. And yet the issue of the gossip about her and Josh weighed heavily on her.

"Emily, dear, you look like you have something on your mind."

Startled at Pastor Adams words, she noticed she'd crushed her apron in her fist. She looked at him as she smoothed it out.

"I've met a few people in my time who had something they needed to say but weren't sure how to go about it." He gestured to a kitchen chair. "Join us. I find many things can be solved with cookies."

She laughed. He was a good man. And the whole town was always glad when he rode in. She had only planned to speak with Maggie, but perhaps he would have wisdom as well.

Taking a seat, she said, "You might have noticed I wasn't in church Sunday."

"Actually, I didn't. There are so many reasons a person may or may not be in church, most of which are none of my business. Being close to God is a lot more than showing up on Sundays."

She nodded. Yes, the women who had been so condemning of her, and Mrs. Luke for supporting her, were regular church attenders.

The back door opened, and she turned. Josh. Lightness filled her chest.

He gave her a smile. "Looks like I'm interrupting a tea party."

Maggie started to stand, but Josh waved her down. "I can get my own coffee. If I'm not intruding."

Pastor Adams looked at Emily and raised his eyebrows.

"Actually, I think it would be helpful if you joined us." She sent him a pleading look. Having him with her would make this easier.

Questions filled his eyes, but he grabbed some coffee and sat at the table.

"I was just beginning to tell Pastor Adams about not being in church Sunday." She hoped this didn't come back to haunt her, but she was going to tell the truth. All the ways it could go wrong flashed through her mind, but she pressed on as her heart sent up a prayer.

Josh nodded at her, his gaze encouraging her.

"Josh had been quite ill. Maggie and I had planned to check on him and bring him food Saturday, but she cut her hand. To make it over the footbridge before dark, I went alone. The water had covered most of it already, but no one had heard from Josh all day. That was worrisome. And when I got to his cabin, I found him lying unconscious on the floor. By the time I got him settled and went to leave, the footbridge was completely inundated, and it was dark out."

"James and I went to help her, but we couldn't get across," Maggie said. "It was too dangerous. I told her to stay put."

Emily flashed her a grateful smile. "The next morning, the bridge was still underwater. Slowly, Josh started to get better." She glanced at her clasped hands in her lap, hoping her face didn't redden as she thought about the thunderstorm and the kiss. "I knew I had to open the schoolhouse the next day, so as soon as the sun was up Monday, I left. The footbridge was still underwater, but I could make it out and the current wasn't too bad. I was able to get across without falling in. Though I'm not sure it was the wisest thing I'd ever done."

"I about had a fit when I saw that she had gone over that footbridge." Josh twirled his mug. "I would have helped her if she'd woken me."

Emily met his gaze. "You were still too sick."

Pastor Adams looked at them. "Seems like you all care for each other very much, risking your lives—and your reputations —to help one another. Sounds like you love your neighbor as yourself, which Jesus called the second greatest commandment. A few people have attempted to come to me with gossip, but I don't listen to it. The Apostle Paul talks about the strife and division gossip can cause, and I can testify to that."

Maggie nodded. "Which was exactly what I told Beth Paige when she came to me."

Pastor Adams gave Maggie a warm smile. "Maybe I'll preach on gossip Sunday."

Panic rose in Emily's chest. She didn't want any attention brought to herself, more than already had been. "Sunday? You'll preach here again on Sunday?" Usually he moved around the area.

Pastor Adams gave Maggie another, unreadable, look. "And every Sunday after that. I've felt since last summer that the Lord was calling me here permanently. The building of the church and schoolhouse, as well as a few other things, confirmed it."

"And we're blessed for it." A soft smile lit Maggie's face. This wasn't news to her; she had already known. So, what other things had confirmed Pastor Adam's calling? Could Maggie be one of them?

"Pastor Adams, that's wonderful. And I have an idea. The teacher's cottage is supposed to be for my use. Josh and his father have fixed it up so it's perfectly habitable. I'm sure the school board would approve your living there instead of me. I can easily stay here at the boardinghouse."

She glanced between Maggie and Pastor Adams. If things were as she suspected, it wouldn't be proper for him to stay here much longer.

"That's very kind of you, Emily. And an answer to prayer, I must say." He shot Maggie a smile. "Not that I don't enjoy the benefits of Maggie's cooking. But for propriety's sake, separate quarters would be ideal."

Emily caught Josh's gaze and swallowed. He knew what she had given up.

"My other thought had been to ask Josh if he'd mind sharing his quarters, but this is a better solution. Thank you, kindly, Emily. I'll speak to Parsons in the next day or so. As to your original question, I would simply advise that gossip will eventually die down if nothing stokes it." He turned to Josh. "And that lies on your shoulders. Consider well what your intentions are with this young woman."

Chapter Nineteen

E mily tapped her fingers on the counter at Fulton's Mercantile. Maggie had a few things for her to pick up, but mostly Emily was there for the mail. Seth had gotten in late last night with it, so if there was something from Silas, it would be here. James and Sally roamed the aisles—they had come directly from school—while Mrs. Fulton filled Maggie's order and retrieved the mail.

She was a bit hesitant to come, knowing that Mrs. Fulton was the center of all the town's goings on, if not outright gossip. But with Pastor Adams and Maggie behind her, she held her head high and reminded herself she was the respectable schoolmarm with nothing to be ashamed of.

Responding automatically to Mrs. Fulton's gossipy prattle, Emily wished she would hurry up. Emily's life could change in the next few minutes depending on if there was a letter.

"I think that does it." Mrs. Fulton placed the last can on the counter.

Emily loaded up her basket. "And the mail?"

"Oh, yes. Just a moment." Mrs. Fulton disappeared behind the wooden partition.

The sound of envelopes sliding across each other grated on Emily's nerves. What was taking her so long?

Mrs. Fulton reappeared. "Four letters for the boardinghouse folk and the latest issue of *Godey's Lady's Book.*"

Emily gave her thanks while she stuffed the mail in the basket with the other items. Calling to James and Sally, they left the store and headed toward the boardinghouse.

Balancing the basket, Emily flipped through the envelopes. One for Maggie, one for Josiah. And two for her. One from Mrs. Luke that she would read tonight when she could savor it.

From the second envelope, Silas's handwriting stared up at her.

The road to the boardinghouse seemed to grow longer instead of shorter, but eventually she made it inside. She dropped the basket of dry goods on the kitchen table, and then ripped open the letter.

Scanning the page, her breath caught. She didn't know what to make of this. She hurried to the barn.

Josh was taking care of the mules, but he looked up when she came in. "You got a letter?"

"Yes, but I don't understand it. Silas says he has no idea what I'm talking about in regards to the money. He'd like to visit, but he's too old to make the trip, so if I want to see him, I'd have to go to Seattle."

"May I see it?"

She thrust it at him. "Maybe you can make sense of it."

He read it then looked up at her. "Are you sure Silas put the money in your bag?"

"I just assumed." She paced. "Where else would it have come from? Given Silas's history, I figured it was him. Now that he says it wasn't him, I have no idea what to think." The whole basis of her actions these last few weeks was a faulty assumption. She could hardly wrap her mind around it.

"Maybe the man who grabbed you put it in your bag somewhere along the way to keep from getting caught with it. It actually makes sense. He knew the money was in your bag. The most likely explanation was that he put it there."

Her head spun. All this time she had assumed it was Silas. She wanted to give him the chance to make things right himself. He had been so angry when she had tried to make amends to the townspeople after she found Jesus. But he'd never lied to her. He hadn't always told her the whole truth, but he'd never misled her when she'd asked him a question directly.

But if it really was the man from the ferry… "What do we do now?"

Josh moved over in front of the tack room and swept the floor with his boot until the knot hole appeared. He reached down and yanked it up, revealing the safe. He opened it and pulled out the money before setting the boards and the floor to rights. "We go see the sheriff."

He shoved the leather bag into a feed sack.

If Silas was lying to her and he was really behind this, there was no turning back now.

Josh was glad Mike Riley was in his office and they didn't have to hunt him down. He was even happier that the man was listening to Emily's story with interest, like he'd hoped Mike would.

Mike leaned back in his chair. "You think this is related to the break-in at the Oregon Express office and Josiah's store?"

Emily nodded.

"Josiah told us his story, but he didn't see the man that hit him," Josh said.

Mike rubbed his chin then reached for the feed sack. He opened the leather pouch and pulled out the bank notes. "Have you counted how much is here?"

Emily shook her head. "I didn't want to know. I just wanted it back to whomever it belongs to."

Mike quickly counted the money. "Five thousand dollars in bank notes from the National Bank of Walla Walla. Seems to me, I remember something about that." He reached for a stack of papers on his desk and flipped through them. "Ah. Is this the guy from the ferry that grabbed you?"

He turned a wanted poster in their direction.

It looked like it could be the man who grabbed Emily, from the glance Josh had gotten. He studied her.

She'd gone pale, fingers to her lips. "Yes. That's him."

The poster said it was Dillon Rogers, part of the Red Dawson Gang, wanted for robbing a payroll delivery of five thousand dollars at the Dexter Horton and Company bank on September 13."

"That's the day before I left Seattle."

"Time line fits." Mike asked her a few more questions, but Josh was stunned by the realization that Mike had taken Emily's word without question, which was more than he himself had done. Because she hadn't told him the whole story, and with good reason, he had immediately assumed the worst.

If she could be so loyal to a man such as Silas, who had badly used her and put her in danger over and over, how might she be to a man who treated her well?

Mike and Emily stood. Josh scrambled to his feet.

"I'll be wiring the marshal about this. I'm sure he'll have some questions for you. I'll have the money locked up in my safe until he gets here." He stared at Josh. "Don't let her out of your sight. This Red Dawson gang is dangerous. In addition to bank robbery, they're wanted for murder."

By CLINGING to Maggie's side and arriving just before the service began—bless Maggie for that—Emily was able to avoid conversation with anyone.

Pastor Adam's sermon wasn't on gossip, but it was on the

Good Samaritan. He also made the announcement that he was taking the pulpit here in Reedsville. At the cheer that went up, Emily was sure Mr. Parsons would have no trouble deciding to turn the teacher's cottage to the pastor's manse. He liked to be on the side of popular opinion.

She thought back to Mrs. Luke's letter that had arrived with Silas's. As usual, she was full of words of encouragement. She was confident that Emily would do well as the school-marm and would win the townspeople over. She also encour-aged Emily to trust Josh. She wished her dear friend could travel to Reedsville to see Emily's life now, but Mrs. Luke had grown frail in recent years, not that one could tell by her lively letters.

After church, while Maggie was in conversation with Bessie White and Emily was searching for Becca, Mr. and Mrs. Parsons cornered her in the churchyard. "I trust the new school year is going well?" Mr. Parsons asked with a peculiar look in his eye. He knew something, and he was going to try and trap her.

"It has been splendid. The children are all eager to learn and have taken to their lessons well." She scanned the crowd. It didn't help being tall if the person she was looking for was as petite as Becca. Seth and Josiah were talking to Josh, but Becca wasn't there. "I expect the rest of the term to go as well."

Mrs. Parsons clutched her husband's arm. "It not only the schoolroom that you must govern, Miss Stanton. Your behavior outside the schoolroom is under examination as well."

She pasted on her best smile. So that was it. "As it should be, ma'am." She met Mrs. Parsons's gaze steadily.

"There has been some disturbing talk—"

Someone bumped into Emily. Becca! She slid her arm through Emily's. "If you'll excuse us? I need to borrow Emily for a moment." She drew Emily away. "I've been looking all over for you."

Once they were a safe distance away and around the corner of the church, Becca lowered her voice. "Josh sent me to rescue you. He thought if he came to get you, it might throw grease on the fire."

Emily smiled at the image. "Considering where they were attempting to steer the conversation, he was right. Thank you so much!"

"Maybe I need to give them something to talk about so they'll forget about you. Back in the day, I was quite a tomboy, running with Seth and Thomas and Josh when they'd let me. Maggie was understanding, but I think I got a talking to about ladylike behavior by nearly every woman in town. They were all relieved when I went off to the university."

Emily giggled. It was difficult to picture elegant Becca running around with the boys.

"I was the opposite. I wanted to have fine dresses and go to tea parties. I used to see the ladies through the window having tea at the hotel. It looked so lovely. They all were delicate and refined, nibbling on their tea cakes and sipping their tea in their lovely dresses and beautiful hats." She sighed. "It seemed like bliss."

Becca nodded. "Last summer, Seth and I took a trip to Portland. I'll tell you the full story sometime, but someone was attempting to harm me and so a trip out of town seemed in order. It was wonderful spending a few days dressing up, shopping, eating at a restaurant. But I can't imagine living in the city."

"I much prefer it here myself." She spotted Josiah, Seth, and Josh walking their way. "Are you enjoying having your father-in-law visit?"

"Josiah is very kind. On that Portland trip I mentioned, he treated me like the father I never had. It's too bad he's leaving soon. But he seems no worse for the bump on his head, and he's eager to get back to his store."

As the men neared, Josh's eyes twinkled and his dimples reappeared. She'd missed that. "The Parsons are headed back to their hotel. I was able to deflect a few of their more pointed questions."

Seth offered Becca his arm. "Maggie's invited us for Sunday dinner. We brought the buggy, so we'll see you there." As they moved off, Becca gave Emily a small wave.

Despite Mr. and Mrs. Parsons and their insinuations, her heart was full and as warm as the sunshine overhead. Having a friend like Becca, well, she'd never had one, so she couldn't quite put into words how wonderful it was to talk and giggle with a woman her own age.

She turned to find Josh staring at her. "Oh, I was lost in thought. Will it be safe for the two of us to be seen walking back to the boardinghouse together?"

He nodded toward his pa with a grin. "We'll have a chaperone."

EMILY AND PA chatted on the way home, but Josh found himself mostly listening. Emily had a nice way with Pa, asking him about Portland and his woodworking. Pa seemed quite taken with her too.

He had to admit, Pa's behavior seemed genuine. When he wasn't drinking, Josh remembered a kind man who was eager to pass on his trade to his son, his only child. But there weren't too many of those memories.

Pa had been eager to go to church today. He was interested in hearing the Word preached and worshipping with the other townsfolk. And during the service, Pa had been attentive. It seemed to be genuine, not just putting on a good face for those around.

It almost seemed too good to be true. If Pa had stopped drinking for good, then Josh might have his father back. He was afraid to hope.

Chapter Twenty

As she was writing the reading assignments on the chalkboard, Emily heard the schoolhouse door open. She turned. Sheriff Riley stood with another man. As soon as she saw his badge, she recognized him. The old fear of seeing lawmen trilled through her body before settling in her stomach. Being around Sheriff Riley had dissipated it some, but these marshals recalled only bad memories from her youth of running from or avoiding lawmen. For good reason.

She looked at the watch pinned to her blouse. It was nearly the end of the school day. The children wouldn't mind getting out a few minutes early. Though if their parents learned why, there would be more fodder for the gossip mill. She suppressed a sigh and nodded at the men.

"Children, please note your reading assignment on the board. Gather your things, and you are dismissed."

The schoolhouse erupted with chatter and movement as the children packed up and streamed out the door around the men, barely giving them a second look.

Emily straightened her desk and stacked her books in an effort to gather her thoughts. She had done nothing wrong, and

Sheriff Riley believed her. But she couldn't help but wish that Josh was there too.

"James?" She waved him up to her desk and lowered her voice. "Please tell your ma and Josh that the sheriff and marshal are here asking me some questions, so I won't be home directly. You go ahead and go home with Sally."

He looked at the men by the door, and his brow furrowed.

"It will be all right. Go along."

As the last child left, the men moved in front of Emily's desk. She recognized him as Portland's marshal who had examined everyone disembarking the ferry in Portland. He was here about the money.

Sheriff Riley turned his hat in his hands. "Miss Stanton, this is Marshal O'Connor. He's been on the trail of the Red Dawson Gang. I wired him about the money you found in your bag. He'd like to ask you a few questions."

She nodded. "Certainly."

Marshal O'Conner pinned her with his gaze. "Why don't you tell us your *story* about how you came upon the money?"

Her heart sank. He didn't believe her. Willing her voice to be calm, she told him about the man on the ferry—who she now knew was Dillon Rogers—and finding the money in her valise. Telling him her suspicions about Silas felt disloyal and sounded ridiculous to her own ears. She finished by explaining about Josh finding the money and their turning it into Sheriff Riley.

Marshal O'Connor turned to Sheriff Riley. "I'd like to take her down to your office for further questions. Frankly, her story sounds like she was the perfect accomplice to the Dawson Gang. Being a woman, she could sneak the money off the ferry without anyone thinking twice." He reached for her arm.

Her feet turned to lead, and pain filled her chest. If she was seen being marched down the street to the sheriff's office like a common criminal, she'd lose her job for sure. Innocent or not, no explanation Maggie or Josh could give would allow her to teach again. Her future shattered around her.

JOSH ENTERED the back of the schoolhouse and heard Emily's voice.

"I'm happy to go with you and answer your questions."

Calm and sure. Which was the opposite of the roiling in his gut ever since he got James's message.

Sheriff Riley stepped forward. "Marshal, I'm sure Miss Stanton will be happy to help in anyway. But I believe her story. It makes sense given the facts. And if she was part of the gang, why would she turn in the money?"

"I never said these folks were smart."

Josh's footsteps rang out as he walked firmly down the aisle. "I think I can be of assistance. I've been with Miss Stanton ever since she found the money. I saw the man grab her."

The marshal turned and studied Josh from boot to hat. "And who might you be?"

As much as Josh would rather land a fist into the man's face, he stuck out his hand. "Josh Benson, owner of the Oregon Express stage line. It was my office that was broken into in Portland. And Josiah Blake was injured when his store was broken into. If she was part of their gang, why would they need to be breaking into places in Portland looking for the money?"

"Maybe she double crossed them."

"And then turned the money into the sheriff?" Josh caught Emily's gaze. Her soft smile reassured him, even though he was trying to reassure her. He reached for her. "Sheriff Riley, if you or the marshal have further questions, we'll be at the boardinghouse"—he turned to the marshal—"as usual."

He tucked Emily's arm through his and escorted her out of the schoolhouse, hoping he was actually coming to her aid and not making things worse.

AFTER SEVERAL DAYS of waiting for the other shoe to drop, Emily incrementally began to relax. The marshal hadn't come by the boardinghouse or the schoolhouse. She was sure it was due to Josh and Sheriff Riley's support.

After school, she arrived the boardinghouse with James and Emily. She was a bit disappointed that Josh hadn't shown up—in fact, she couldn't see him in the yard or the corral—but considering the last few times he'd brought bad news, relief was probably the better emotion.

While James and Sally hurried off to chores, Maggie handed Emily a mug of coffee. "Any further word from the sheriff or the marshal?"

"No, thank goodness." She sank into the kitchen chair.

"The marshal came by today to talk to Josh. Sounded like his story corroborated yours. But the marshal is staying in town which means—"

Her heart sank. "He's staying at the Parsons's hotel."

Maggie nodded. She put a hand on Emily's shoulder. "Don't listen to what others say. The folks that know you the best—me and my children, Josh, Seth, and Becca, not to mention Charles and Josiah—we all know who you are in here." She laid a plump finger over Emily's heart.

Emily's eyes teared up. "But if I lose my job—"

"Then we'll figure something out. But don't go borrowing trouble."

A knock at the front door caused a frown to furrow Maggie's brow. She left the kitchen and went to the front door.

Emily took a sip of her coffee. *Lord, why is it so hard to separate from my past? When will I ever truly feel like a new creation?* She would write Mrs. Luke back and ask her. She had to admit she was blessed to have women like Maggie, Mrs. Luke, and Becca in her life. Shouldn't that be enough?

Voices from the front of the house drifted into the kitchen, and Maggie returned. "Mr. Parsons is here to see you. He's in the parlor." Her face didn't give anything away, but Mr. Parsons showing up couldn't mean anything good.

She moved into the parlor on leaden feet.

Mr. Parsons stood inside, twisting his hat in his hands. "Miss Stanton. It has come to my attention that the Portland marshal is here investigating you in regards to a payroll robbery."

"That's not actually—"

"We expect our teachers to be a moral example to our children. First, questions about your propriety, and now this. It's simply not acceptable."

"Mr. Parsons—"

"This is not open to discussion. Whether the insinuations are true is of no matter at this point. A teacher has answered our ad and will be replacing you. You may stay on for two more weeks until she arrives."

Her bones turned to jelly, and she fought the urge to collapse on the settee. Words failed her, but even if she could defend herself, apparently it didn't matter. She was being replaced.

Mr. Parsons put on his hat. "And by the by, you had no business offering the teacher's cottage to Pastor Adams. It will be housing for the next teacher. If the town wants Pastor Adams to have a manse, they can raise the funds for it. Good day, Miss Stanton." He let himself out.

She sunk onto the settee and covered her face. She couldn't believe it. She assumed once she was in the position and doing a good job, they would let her keep teaching. She never once imagined being fired.

Now what?

The settee dipped next to her as someone sat down. Probably Maggie.

Someone touched her shoulder. The smell of horses and hay wafted past her. Definitely not Maggie. She lowered her hands.

"I saw Parsons leave. He told me what happened. If it would

make you feel any better, I could go punch him." A dimple punctured Josh's cheek.

She gave him a small smile. "I wish it were that simple."

"Mr. Parsons is only one school board member. Sure, he's the president, but if you could convince the other members that you were the best teacher, they could overrule him."

She stared at him then shook her head. "They probably think the same way he does."

"You'll never know unless you try."

She didn't really believe there was any hope, there never had been for a girl like her. But it was kind of Josh to care and try to help. "What do you suggest?"

"We're on the edge of the wilderness and not much cultural happens here. Last year, Mrs. Parsons, Mrs. Fulton, and Cassandra Parsons—now O'Malley—put together an Evening of Culture and a Valentine's box supper. It brought the town together and gave them something to do. If you could put on an event that would bring the whole town out, they'd riot before they'd let Parsons fire you."

She slowly nodded. Then remembered. "I only have two weeks! What can I put together in that time? If it were Christmas, we could do a pageant."

"How about a harvest festival?" Maggie stood in the doorway. "Becca and I can help you plan it. Between the three of us, we can come up with plenty of ideas."

Emily wrapped her arms around her middle. It was sweet how they were all trying to help her. She couldn't believe she had such good friends. Her heart was bruised, but it was still beating thanks to the love and kindness they'd all shown her.

It was a good idea. It wouldn't allow her to keep her job, that she was sure of, but it would be her way of giving back to the town, leaving them with an enjoyable experience. And for a small moment in time, she could be a part of them.

She was going to miss them all when she had to return to Portland in two weeks.

A VOLLEY of ideas flew across the table at supper. Josh was surprised at how excited Pa was with the project. He volunteered to build booths for games and for treats.

"I know how to swing a hammer, and I have some free time on my hands. Emily, don't you worry. This will be a bang-up festival." Pa punctuated his statement with a mild slap on the table.

Maggie talked about baking treats and asking the farmers to bring their wares in. "Speak to the O'Malley boys. Sy's off at Willamette University, so he can't provide music, but Stephen makes cakes that I'd be proud to call my own. And their apple trees are ready to be harvested. I'm sure they'd be happy to supply some for games and treats."

Sally piped up. "There should be music and dancing."

"I can open the event with prayer and give a short devotional. Folks will know that I've given this event my blessing." Pastor Adams nodded at Emily. "I hope that helps you."

"Thank you, Pastor Adams. I truly appreciate it. Especially after I cost you your housing."

"The Lord has a way of working things out. I'll be bunking with Josh and Charlie. Maggie has kindly allowed me to take my meals here, so you see, the situation is even better." His eyes twinkled, and he cast a wink at Maggie which had her cheeks pinking up.

Emily hid her smile. "And how am I going to make this educational?"

"Put on a play reenacting the founding of Reedsville," Josh volunteered. Emily's gaze swung his way, and he swallowed. The hope in her eyes lit a fire in his chest. And he didn't want to see that hope dim.

"That's a fabulous idea. Thank you, Josh. Who would I talk to about that?"

"I can help you. I know most of it, and there are a few of the old-timers that you can interview. But Maggie here is a great source."

Maggie nodded. "That's a good idea, Josh. And I think it wouldn't be remiss to include each of the school board members' families as part of that history. Everyone likes to have their contribution noticed."

Watching Emily's face, Josh thought he saw the first glimmer of hope. He was leaving for a mail run early in the morning. Josiah was riding with him back to Portland. While the marshal was in town, Emily was probably safe from the gang, but possibly not from the marshal. Still, it seemed like he'd already done his damage. He opened and closed his fist at the thought.

Pa had promised to keep an eye on Emily. He had spent most of the day working on a bookcase for her with a cupboard at the top. Things were certainly strange when he was trusting Pa to look out for someone he cared about.

Chapter Twenty-One

J osh was up early, saddling the mules, when a buggy pulled up with Seth, Becca, and Josiah. Josiah grabbed his bag and hopped out of the buggy then shook Seth's hand. "I'll be back for the harvest festival. Can't miss those big doings."

"You're welcome to stay any time." Becca gave him a hug. "We love having you."

"I've greatly enjoyed my stay, but I have to get back and see what Jake has done with my store."

Josh and Josiah waved as Seth and Becca pulled away. Josiah loaded up his horse, and they mounted up and were on their way.

Once they were out of town, Josiah spoke up. "Thanks for letting this old man ride with you."

"I'm grateful for the company, even if it's only one way. I appreciate you bringing Pa out here with you. Admittedly, that's not something I ever thought I'd say."

"I think it was the other way around. My noggin was pretty sore, and it was probably a good idea for me to have someone join me on the trip. He's good company. He comes into the store quite often, and we have coffee and jaw about things."

He turned and looked at Josiah. "I didn't know that. Actually, that surprises me."

"I know he wasn't much of a pa to you growing up. And he regrets that mightily. I know he didn't intend to become a drunk. He didn't understand the power of drink when he turned to it to dull the pain in his leg."

Josh nodded. His head knew that. His heart had a more difficult time with it. But he'd always thought Pa was embarrassed to be around Josiah since Josiah knew the truth about things and practically raised Josh.

Josiah had shown Pa grace. He let that thought roll around his head for a bit.

They swapped out mail bags in Oregon City and then headed into Portland. Josh headed to the livery to get the mules settled, and Josiah headed to his store. Later when Josh walked into the store, Josiah and Jake had their heads bent going over the books.

Josh waved to him but was glad Josiah was busy. He wanted to look around a bit. There was something he needed to do.

After wandering the aisles, he found himself at a glass display case by the front counter that contained pins, rings, bracelets, earbobs, and necklaces. He remembered what Emily had said to Mike about not owning any jewelry. Every woman needed a piece of jewelry. Isn't that what they dreamed about? He studied the case, hating the feeling of uncertainty that rolled through his gut. He knew nothing about jewelry or what Emily would like. His eyes wandered over the wares, and he shook his head. He wished Maggie were here.

Josiah came over. Josh's ears heated, and he opened his mouth, not sure what he was going to say.

But seemingly like magic, Josiah reached into the case and pulled out a delicately engraved oval locket with a fine gold chain draped over his hands. "It's quite elegant without being ostentatious. And see?" He sprung a small latch, and the front of the locket clicked open. "She can put a small photograph or a lock of hair in here." I think it'll be just perfect." He winked.

Josh rubbed the back of his neck. If Josiah, who hadn't been around the boardinghouse much, knew of Josh's feelings for Emily, did everyone? Probably. As that thought sunk in, another one came fast after it. Did Emily?

Josiah smiled at him. "Shall I wrap it for you?"

"Yes." He didn't hesitate. She deserved something as delicate and beautiful as she was. He would give it to her the night of the harvest festival.

And tell her how he felt about her. Make her see that she still had a future—with him—even if she lost her teaching job.

AFTER SCHOOL, footsteps sounded behind Emily, and she turned. The marshal was back. The boardinghouse was in sight, so Emily sent Sally and James on ahead to get started on their chores. James dragged his feet, but did as he was told, his head turning back to Emily frequently.

"Marshal O'Connor. What a surprise. What brings you out this way?" She kept her voice even, though she wondered if he could see her heart beating through her bodice. She forced a smile. No point in antagonizing the man.

"I've brought you a warning, in case you didn't heed my earlier words. While Sheriff Riley and that Josh Benson think your explanations make perfect sense, I think it just shows how much you've got them wrapped up under your influence. After talking to Mr. Parsons and staying in his comfortable establishment, I've heard about your exploits around town and the hints of scandal that already follow you."

How dare he! The urge to stomp her foot and argue almost overpowered her, but it would just play into the image he already had. Instead, she imagined she was one of the ladies she'd seen through the hotel window having tea and this was simply an annoying conversation. She lifted her chin. "I'm sorry you don't believe me, but I've told you nothing but the truth."

He pointed his finger at her. "I'm heading back to Portland. But don't believe for a minute that this issue is settled. It won't be settled until the whole Dawson Gang is behind bars. And I wouldn't hesitate to put a woman there, either." He swiveled on his heel and walked away, whistling.

She clasped her hands together to keep them from shaking. He wasn't convinced of her innocence, but he didn't have any evidence against her and he was leaving. On the whole, the news was good. When she had to relocate to Portland, she hoped she never ran into him.

She entered the back door of the boardinghouse and removed her hat.

Becca sat at the kitchen table drinking tea. She stood and hugged Emily.

"What a nice surprise! Just let me run upstairs and put my things away." Emily hurried up and back down the stairs and when she had returned, Maggie had a tea cup in front of Emily's place and a plate of cookies. It reminded her so much of a tea party she had to blink back tears as she lowered herself into her chair.

Becca squeezed her hand. "While you've been teaching, Maggie and I have been busy. We called on most of the ladies in town, and they are going to bring baked goods and preserves. We'll have a small contest with the mayor and the sheriff as judges. Some of the goods will be used as prizes for games, some will be auctioned to raise money for more school books, and some will be sold. Ben, who runs the telegraph and the Oregon Express office, will sell tickets for us."

"Did Mr. Parsons agree to this?"

Becca nearly squealed. "That's the best part. I talked to Mrs. Parsons because she loves social events. I had her thinking this was nearly her idea, a follow up to the Valentine's Day box supper. She loved that her husband the mayor 'as the most important man in town'—her words—would be the judge. We didn't even have to talk to him. She'll convince him to do it."

Emily shook her head, amazed at these ladies as they continued to talk about their plans for games and prizes, music and dancing. Becca had a whole list made.

"Thank you so much for this. I can't even begin to repay you." Emily reached for Becca's hand and squeezed it.

"Nonsense. This gives me something to do, and I want to help you. You're my friend, and I need you to stay in Reedsville. My motives are highly selfish."

Emily didn't believe Becca had a selfish bone in her body, but whatever her reasons, Emily was deeply grateful. She'd never been so loved.

But Becca was mistaken in one thing: Emily couldn't stay in Reedsville.

BONE TIRED, Josh trudged to his cabin after getting the mules settled for the night, Emily's gift carefully wrapped and tucked safely in his breast pocket. The road had been dry when he'd crossed it both ways, so it was ready to be cleared now. Seth had made good progress rebuilding the logging camp so maybe he could spare some men, and they could get the road repaired and the stage line running again. It'd be a sight better than mule skinning. Plus, it'd bring in more money. And none too soon.

There was a lamp burning, so Pa must still be up. Or Pastor Adams. Roy, as the man asked to be called. He entered the cabin.

"Pa?" He wasn't in the main room.

Josh looked in the kitchen. Pa sprawled on the floor, unconscious. "Pa!"

He rushed over and knelt, his stomach rolling. Was this how Emily felt when she'd found him? He hated that she'd had those same feelings.

The smell of booze was strong. His eyes watered, and he coughed.

Disbelief warred with the certainty that a drunk would never change. Yet he'd thought Pa had. Things had been good between them. Josh was beginning to trust him again. Now he wanted to drag him out and dunk his head in the creek.

He scanned the room. There weren't any booze bottles. Maybe Pa had been at the saloon? And somehow managed to get home and then pass out? He didn't want to think about it. He looked at Pa one more time. Hauling him up to the loft to his bed was not something Josh wanted to do. He didn't want to wake up Roy. If he was honest, he didn't want Roy seeing Pa like this. Roy was probably different, but he didn't want to test the theory.

He wasn't going to give up his own bed. From the trunk at the foot of his bed, he grabbed an extra blanket and covered Pa with it. If he was still on the floor when Roy came down in the morning, he could do his own explaining.

Chapter Twenty-Two

S nores awoke Josh too early the next morning. Gray light was just spilling through the front windows. Pa was on his back in the kitchen snoring up a storm. He was surprised the rafters weren't shaking, and Roy hadn't come downstairs to witness the disturbance.

Anger propelled Josh out of bed. He lit the stove, washed up, and got dressed. Soon it was hot enough to set on the coffee pot. Pa would need it.

Josh stepped over Pa as he made his way around the kitchen, but finally nudged him with the toe of his boot. "Pa! Get up."

The snores stopped, followed by a little moaning, but Pa didn't waken.

Josh bent down and shook him.

"Wha—what's going on?" Pa lifted his head and looked around. "Why am I in the kitchen?"

"Might have something to do with what you were drinking last night."

Pa sat up. "I wasn't drinking anything." He grabbed his head. "At least, I don't remember." His shoulders slumped. "Honest, son, I had supper at Maggie's and stayed in her parlor talking to

James about how things used to be before the West got all civilized. Then Roy and I came home."

"There's a few things you left out. Where's the bottle?"

"What bottle?" Pa grabbed his head but pushed to his feet and pulled out a kitchen chair and sat. "That coffee about ready?" He pressed his hands into his back. "I am too old to be sleeping on the floor."

"Pa, you smelled like a saloon when I came home last night. You've been drinking. You told me you'd changed." Josh poured two mugs, slammed the coffee pot down, and slopped the cups on the table.

At his actions, a bottle tipped over on the shelf next to the stove. He picked it up. "What's this?" He popped the cork off and sniffed. The sharp smell made his eyes water. He corked it back up.

"I got that at the mercantile. That old injury in my leg has been paining me." Pa sipped his coffee.

Josh looked at the label. DR. KILMER'S SWAMP ROOT. Given the list on the label of what the product could cure, it seemed to be just what you would need for anything. The bottle was half empty. "Did you take all this last night?"

Pa squinted. "Didn't think I'd had that much. Just kept sipping on it. But I guess I did."

Roy appeared in the kitchen, his usually combed-back dark hair in disarray. "Morning, boys. Any coffee ready? I slept like the dead last night."

Josh poured him a mug and handed it over.

"Thank you. Charlie, how's that leg feeling?" He swallowed the coffee.

"A lot better than my head." Which was propped up by his hands.

"That Swamp Root stuff didn't work?" Roy studied Pa over the rim of his mug, his gaze sympathetic, not judgmental.

Josh cut a glance at Roy. He wasn't sure what to make of the pastor's reaction. He tapped Pa on the shoulder. "Finish your coffee. We'll have breakfast at Maggie's."

THE SIGHT of Josh walking into the dining room fluttered Emily's heart. She assumed he'd gotten in late last night, so she wasn't sure if she'd see him this morning, but it was good to see for herself that he had returned safely. His chocolate eyes warmed her heart.

His pa and Pastor Adams followed him in and settled around Maggie's table.

"How was your trip?" Such common words, but she hoped her smile conveyed her genuine concern and affection.

"Good. Josiah got home safely, and the road is dried out. I'll talk to Seth today about getting it cleared, but the stage should start running again this week."

"I'm glad to hear it." She wished she could linger, but it was clear his pa was ailing. He had barely touched the big breakfast Maggie had set before him, mostly sipping coffee and nibbling on a biscuit. Pastor Adams had no such reserve, digging in heartily.

She had to get off to school. She rushed upstairs to grab her things, came back down, and called for Sally and James. They had just stepped out the back door when Josh called her name. She turned to Sally. "Go around to the front of the boarding-house. I'll catch up."

Josh's large, rough, warm hand engulfed hers.

"I'm glad you're back and home safe."

"Me too." He paused. "It's not quite the harvest moon yet, but it's getting closer. Want to take a walk with me after supper?"

She squeezed his hand. "I'd like that a lot."

"Good."

She turned and hurried down the back steps, catching a glimpse of him staring after her as she rounded the corner of the boardinghouse. Her heart beat fast in her chest, and it wasn't because of her quickened steps. Her feelings were all tangled up with Josh's, and she didn't see a good way forward. Her teaching job was ending, and she would have to go back to Portland and ask Mrs. Hanson for her old job back.

She considered asking Maggie for a job as well. Right now Emily was mostly in the way, but when the stage started running would Maggie need a hand? Usually Becca helped her, and Emily didn't want to be a charity case.

No, she would have to return to Portland. But maybe she could see Josh when he came to town weekly on the stage runs. That thought gave her a bit of hope. Yet she held it lightly. Not one of her plans had survived, so she was afraid to put too much weight on such a fragile expectation.

EMILY WAS a sight for sore eyes, looking as pretty as spring in that pink dress of hers that Josh favored. He thought about the gift he had for her. Snatching a few minutes with her before she headed off to school was a spontaneous thought. He was searching for anything that gave them more time together.

He stepped back into the kitchen and pulled out the bottle of Dr. Kilmer's Swamp Root. He showed it to Maggie. "Is this stuff any good? I found Pa passed out on the floor last night smelling like a saloon. He swears he wasn't drinking, but that he was here."

"He was." Maggie took the bottle, uncorked it, and sniffed it. She jerked away. "I saw him drinking that last night while he was talking to James and Roy. I offered him willow bark tea since his leg was hurting, but he said he didn't want to be a bother." She pulled a box out of a cupboard. "I don't much hold with patent medicines. That one smells like pure moonshine. I'll make him some willow bark tea. It'll help his head today too. And I'll send him home with a poultice for tonight."

Relief slid across his shoulders, and the faint flicker of hope grew larger. So Pa had been telling the truth. Maybe he had changed. Time would tell. The lightness in his chest returned.

She patted Josh's arm. "Don't be too hard on him." She tilted her head to meet his gaze. "Or yourself."

He mulled over Maggie's words while he did his chores. But the package sitting on his trunk at home and the pretty woman in pink were more preferable thoughts.

EMILY HAD HARDLY TASTED her supper and was glad when it was over. The whole day had been one big distraction. There had been a letter from Mrs. Luke when she got home from school. Emily had written about losing her teaching job and the plans for the harvest festival. She had inquired if Mrs. Luke knew of any work in her town. If she had to leave Reedsville, then maybe she should relocate where she had a friend instead of assuming she had to return to Portland.

Instead, Mrs. Luke had encouraged her to stay in Reedsville with the community of friends she had already established. She reassured Emily that no one would consider her a charity case and the gossip would fade away. There was a gentle reminder that Emily didn't always have to run when things didn't go as planned, that she could stay and see what other potential plans God might have in store for her.

She didn't know what to make of it. It seemed impossible. And yet she trusted Mrs. Luke.

She carried supper plates to the kitchen and began ladling hot water from the stove reservoir into the washbasin and turned her mind to her walk with Josh tonight.

What would they talk about? They hadn't had a real conversation since he'd found the money. He'd rescued her from the marshal, who'd finally gone back to Portland, though not without emphasizing that he didn't believe her. And he'd come up with the harvest festival idea. But something had shifted between them.

Before she could begin shaving the soap, Maggie chased her off. "Go on. I can manage this. Once the stage starts running, I'll need your help."

Maggie meant well, knowing that Emily wanted to feel useful and earn her keep, and Maggie was providing that so Emily could stay in Reedsville. But could she stay in a town where she was the disgraced, fired schoolmarm? Where she lived off the charity of others? How would she ever be a respected citizen?

"Ready?" Josh stood behind her in the kitchen where she hadn't moved.

And yet, there was this man, the one who made her heart feel things she never dreamed of. She met his gaze and suppressed a shiver at its intensity. "Yes. I don't even think I'll need my shawl, it's a warm enough night."

They stepped outside and headed toward Becca and Seth's place. She was grateful. Parading in front of the town with Josh couldn't possibly make her reputation worse, but it could hurt his.

"It sounds like Becca and Maggie have been busy helping with the harvest festival." Josh set an easy pace that her long legs had no trouble keeping up with.

"Yes. I'm so grateful. I never would have had time to do it all myself after school. And I don't know that I would have been welcomed as warmly."

The gibbous moon lit their path clearly.

"Are you looking forward to the harvest festival?"

She clasped her hands together. "I have mixed emotions. The festival itself is a splendid idea, and I think the town will truly enjoy it. I just wish it wasn't my swan song."

Josh stopped and turned to face her, wrapping her hands in his own. "Don't give up, Emily. We all believe that this harvest festival will prove to the townspeople what a treasure you truly are." His gaze met hers, the moonlight casting shadows across his face. "We all want you to stay." He paused. "I want you to stay." He brushed an escaped tendril off her cheek. "Go with me to the harvest party?"

Her heart pounded as if it would burst through her shirt-waist. "I'd like nothing better."

He lowered his head, his lips brushing hers lightly at first and then with more intensity. She poured all her hopes and dreams about the future into her kiss, not wanting this moment to end, wishing that it meant everything would be fine. A glimmer of hope fanned to life in her chest.

Chapter Twenty-Three

T he sun was just peeking over the ridge when Josh, Pa, Seth, Roy and a group of men from the logging camp made their way to the mudslide. The weight resting on Josh's shoulders slipped off a bit more as they got closer. He had been rid of that cough and was back to full strength. He was going to get his stage line up and running.

And Emily was going to the harvest festival with him.

He and Pa hadn't talked about the patent medicine disaster. But they had an easy, working relationship. Which is more than they'd ever had.

The men labored hard all day. Clearing the mud, rocks, trees, and debris left them all tired and hungry. Maggie had packed a substantial lunch, but they demolished it. By the time the sun headed toward the western horizon, the road was better than it had been. They used the rocks and bigger tree trunks to shore up the mountainside, to keep the hill in place until the vegetation grew back next spring.

On the ride back, all Josh thought about was food and a bath. He couldn't figure out which he'd rather have first.

Pa pulled his horse next to him. "Remember that fancy

toolbox I used to have, the one with all the drawers and compartments?"

Josh nodded. He remembered it well. When he was a boy, he loved playing with the drawers and slots, a place for everything. He also remembered, with a pang in his heart, having to sell it to Josiah to pay for Ma's medicine. It was the last thing of Pa's he had sold, and it had brought in the most money. Why was Pa bringing this up now?

"I've been noodling on it some. I saw an ad for an even fancier one in one of those catalogues Josiah has. With the two of us working together, I think we can build one. What do you think?"

His throat tightened, and he had to swallow. This was Pa's way of apologizing. And he wanted to take it. Forgive Pa, for everything, and move forward. "Yeah. Yeah, I do. I think it's a great idea."

"Something I noticed about this town. There's a lot of people that come through here. Some stay, some move on. But most of them don't have things like bedsteads, tables, and chairs. Those are a bit hard to tote across the country. If you don't mind me hanging around, I figure I could set up a good business making those things for folks. And when you're not running your stage, you could help me."

Josh blinked. Dratted dusty trail. "I think that's a fine idea, Pa."

EMILY FLIPPED through the dresses on the pegs. For the tenth time. It didn't change anything. She didn't have anything appropriate to wear to the harvest festival. Simple shirtwaists and skirts for teaching. Her one pink dress. Her wool traveling dress. The valise didn't hold much, which was fine because she didn't own much.

But she wanted the harvest festival to be special. Josh was

escorting her, and she wanted him—and herself—to be able to hold their heads high when the townspeople started gossiping.

Could she make a dress in time for the festival? She had to try.

Skewering her hat to her head, she grabbed her reticule and headed down to Fulton's Mercantile. No time like the present to confront gossip.

Once inside, she nodded to Mrs. Fulton, who was busy helping someone else. She headed to the fabrics. Pastels always looked good on her with her pale skin and hair. She found a buttery yellow calico with blue-sprigged flowers. A bit of lace and some deep blue buttons completed her pile.

Mrs. Fulton stepped over. "I think that's a lovely choice." She held up a length of fabric to Emily's face. "So pretty with your delicate coloring."

"Th-thank you." She was a bit taken a back. Mrs. Fulton's kindness wasn't what she had steeled herself for.

Mrs. Fulton looked at the other items Emily had selected. "You have an eye for these things. Do you need anything else?"

She shook her head and followed Mrs. Fulton to the counter.

The bell above the door rang just as Emily was completing her purchase. She turned to see Mrs. Parsons enter.

Mrs. Parsons smiled at Mrs. Fulton, then caught sight of Emily. Her face hardened. Her gaze slid to Emily's purchases, and her lips pursed. "Mrs. Fulton, I see you're busy. I'll just browse until you're available."

Mrs. Fulton met Emily's gaze, and to her surprise, her eyes were kind. "It'll be a lovely dress, dear. For the harvest festival?"

"Yes, if I can finish it in time."

Mrs. Fulton patted her hand. "You'll do just fine."

Emily turned and made her way to the door, pushing it open to leave the store, but not before noticing the daggers Mrs. Parsons shot her way, nor the way she hurried over to whisper to Mrs. Fulton.

EMILY WORKED every night on her dress, since she didn't have any future lesson planning to do. During the day, Maggie and Sally would take turns basting in the cut pieces or sewing up the finished seams. With these ladies on her side, who cared what women like Mrs. Parsons thought? Nobody had run her out of town on a rail. And even though there had been gossip, there probably always would be. The people who cared about her knew who she truly was.

Finished attaching the skirt to the bodice, she hurried up to her room to try it on. The looking glass over her washstand reflected a lady. She nodded to her reflection. *Yes, I am.*

Holding up the unfinished hem, she moved downstairs to the parlor.

"It looks lovely, Emily. You did a beautiful job." Maggie knelt on the floor and motioned Emily forward so she could pin the hem.

"I couldn't have done it without you and Sally helping. And Becca practically running the harvest festival."

"Turn." Maggie spoke around a mouthful of pins.

She made a half turn.

Maggie pulled the pins out of her mouth and stuck them in the fabric as she worked. "You'll find that's true about everything in life. As much as we'd like to think we're independent and self-sufficient, we really can't get along without help. We need each other." Maggie sat back on her haunches to examine her work. "And that's a good thing. The Bible calls us the body of Christ, not individuals." She shook her head and met Emily's gaze. "The dress is truly lovely, Emily. But far more beautiful is the young lady in it."

JOSH PULLED the stagecoach into Reedsville, successfully completing the first run since the road was fixed. Mr. Parsons was pacing the sidewalk in front of the Oregon Express office. Which confirmed Josh's suspicion that the woman on his stage was the replacement teacher.

She had done nothing but complain the whole trip. When she'd boarded, she'd been upset to find Reedsville a full day's stagecoach ride from Portland. She'd been informed it was only a short distance and seemed to blame Josh for the misunderstanding. She hated the bumping and jostling, asking at the way station if he could make things go more smoothly.

Old Ben came out of the office, slightly hunched over from his rheumatism, to put the step down and help the passengers disembark. Josh heard the woman's complaining before he could see her face.

"Are you Mr. Parsons? Do you think it's amusing to describe this town as *near* to Portland?" She emerged from the stage and headed for Parsons, who took a step back with widened eyes.

"Uh, yes—"

"What kind of fool thinks that a stagecoach is an appropriate way to travel anywhere? And what kind of town is this?" She peered up and down the street. "It's nothing like the innovative, forward-thinking town you described in your ad for the teaching position. It's a misrepresentation is what it is." The feather on her hat bobbed for emphasis.

Ben handed her a valise. "Miss, is this yours?"

She snatched it away. "What kind of accommodations have you provided for me?"

"There's a small teacher's cottage near the school. I can take you there now." Parsons stuck out his elbow to escort her down the street.

Her voice faded only slightly as she continued berating Parsons.

Josiah stepped out of the stage last. He'd kept his word and returned for the harvest festival. He looked up and tipped his hat to Josh with a grin. Poor man had been subject to the woman's complaining the whole trip.

Josh pulled the stage down to the barn with a grin. If that was Emily's replacement, he didn't think Emily had too much to worry about.

Chapter Twenty-Four

E mily smoothed down the yellow calico and checked her hair one more time in the mirror. Everyone from the boardinghouse and many of the townspeople had all helped set up the booths since early morning. The children had decorated the schoolhouse as part of their school day Friday. She had blinked back tears as she had spent time telling each child what she noticed about their strengths and gifts. If this was the last time she'd be their teacher, she wanted each of them to know how special she found them.

And now it was time. She hurried down, stopping two stairs before the end. Josh stood at the bottom in a suit, looking as handsome as she'd ever seen him. Her mouth went dry.

"Emily, you look beautiful." He held his hand out to her, and she took it, stepping down the rest of the stairs. He led her into the parlor.

She floated, as if the ground wasn't really there. His gaze never left her, and her cheeks grew warm. Any casualness between then was gone, replaced by this new intensity.

He placed a small, wrapped package in her hand. "This is for you."

She stared at him. Why was he giving her a gift?

He motioned for her to open it.

No, she was leaving. On the stage he would be driving. She pushed it back in his direction. "I can't—"

"Yes, you can. I want you to." He pushed it back toward her. "But—"

"Open it. Please?" His eyes were soft. She couldn't deny him.

She undid the paper and found a golden locket with a delicate chain. "Oh, it's lovely! I've never seen anything so fine."

"Let me put it on you." He took the chain from her fingers and fastened it around her neck, his fingers brushing the back of her neck, sending tingles down her spine.

"Thank you, Josh. It goes perfectly with my dress." She fingered the locket. If only she could put an image of him in there. "I've never owned anything so lovely. But why?"

He brushed his fingers across her cheek. "A lady as pretty as you deserves something special." He leaned in and feathered a kiss across her lips. "May I escort you to the harvest festival?" He tucked her hand under his arm.

Emily's heart melted. Josh was being so wonderful just when he knew she needed it, giving her the strength and grace to face her last act as the town's teacher. She couldn't imagine loving him anymore than she did right now.

Which would make leaving all the more painful.

THE CHILDREN KICKED off the festivities with their play on the town's founding, which had delighted all the townspeople, especially those whose names were mentioned as founding families.

Pastor Adams gave a devotional on the various gifts of the body of Christ and led them in prayer. Then the musicians took the stage and the music started. The booths opened, and the festival began.

Music filled the air, and Emily laughed and whirled as Josh spun her around among the other couples in the Virginia Reel.

She had never had so much fun in her life. And everyone seemed to be enjoying themselves. Many people had thanked her for doing something so nice for the town.

As the dance ended, Josh led her to the edge, and she caught her breath.

He nodded toward a petite woman with a full figure and a stylish traveling suit talking to Mrs. Parsons and gesturing as she spoke. "That's the schoolteacher Parsons hired. But I don't think you have too much to worry about."

"Why would you say that?"

"Let's just say she didn't think Parsons was honest in his description of our fair town, and she's looking for something more citified."

Emily raised her eyebrows. Reedsville wasn't for everyone, but it held the people she loved the most. Especially this man here. The meaning of his words sunk in. She studied the woman, who certainly seemed to be expressing her many opinions to Mrs. Parsons, who couldn't get a word in edgewise. If this teacher didn't work out, Emily possibly still had a job. At least for a while longer.

"Would you like some punch?" Josh touched her arm, sending heat through her dress sleeve.

"Yes, thank you."

"I'll be right back." He moved off.

She took a few slow steps in the direction of the new schoolteacher, while watching the dancers begin the next dance. Pastor Adams had escorted Maggie to the dance floor, and Josiah was leading Becca.

The teacher-to-be's shrill voice carried. "I was completely ill from all the rocking and jostling. Not to mention the dust. I don't know why anyone thinks that is an appropriate form of transportation for gentlefolk. And the cottage!" She waved a lacy handkerchief in front of her face. "How could anyone conceive of living there? It's a hovel. It's fortunate I insisted on being put up in the hotel until I can return to civilization. Unfortunately, I have to travel on that infernal contraption to get out of this place."

Emily covered her mouth and laughed. Oh my. No, that woman would not last long here, even if she were willing to give it a try.

"Well, I wish you'd reconsider." Mrs. Parsons said. "Our current teacher is just unsuitable. Portland's marshal came looking for her in regards to a payroll robbery, which she might have been an accomplice to. And there are rumors she spent the night at the stagecoach driver's cabin. No one saw them, but neither were at church on Sunday. One can only draw one's own conclusions. So you can see why we can't have someone of that character teaching our children."

"Well, I'm sorry you—"

Emily didn't stay to hear the rest of the teacher's response. She hurried away, blinking back tears. She knew Mrs. Parsons gossiped about her. It just felt like a horse kick to the stomach to actually hear her say those things to someone else.

The worst of it was, it was all true. And yet, it wasn't. At least not the way Mrs. Parsons was implying it was.

Emily moved around the corner of the schoolhouse. She'd get a bit of air and get her tears under control before returning to the party. The people that knew her and loved her knew that everything she'd done had only been motivated by thoughts for others. Not for herself. She just wished she could prove it somehow.

She dabbed at her tears when a familiar-but-unwelcome scent wafted by. She spun, just to have someone grab her arms and a hand clamp over her mouth.

JOSH CARRIED two cups of punch in his hands. He'd been waylaid by Mike Riley, who'd given him the latest update on the Red Dawson Gang and Dillon Rogers. Which wasn't much.

Other than reports they had been heading south, probably to California. He'd been grateful for the update, but eager to get back to Emily. He'd never seen her so happy.

She wasn't where he'd left her. But that wasn't a surprise considering how long he'd been gone. People had been coming to talk to her all night. He moved around the dancers and studied the whole yard. He was heading for the booths when Mrs. Parsons stopped him.

He spoke before she could. He didn't want to hear anything she had to say. "Have you seen Miss Stanton in the last few minutes? I have punch for her." Which might have been one of the dumbest things he'd ever said.

"No, but actually, that's what I'd like to talk to you about."

"I really need—"

"I've known you a long time, Josh. I don't think your spending time with her is helping your reputation. You know what folks are saying, don't you?"

"Ma'am, with all respect, I don't care. Emily is one of the kindest, most selfless, strongest people I know. I'm honored that she wants to spend time with me. And anyone who truly knows her will say the same thing. Just look at this event. The whole town is here raising money for the school and having a good time. Considering the way she's been treated, I'd say this festival shows just how kind and considerate she really is. Now if you'll excuse me." He headed toward the booths, not really seeing where he was going. Once far enough away from Mrs. Parsons, he took a few deep breaths. It wouldn't do to let Emily see him upset. He didn't want anything to ruin her night.

Chapter Twenty-Five

Dillon Rogers. Emily would recognize that awful scent anywhere.

He dragged her back through the woods, his hand firmly over her mouth.

She fought rising panic as she tried to get enough air through her nose. She squirmed and kicked, thrashing out behind her, trying to make contact with any part of his body.

But he was wary of all her moves and kept out of her way without loosening his grip over her mouth. After what felt like forever, they stopped. She was sure they were too far away for anyone to hear her scream.

Every sense strained trying to find any clue in the dark woods that would help her. A wild animal would be preferable to the man who held her captive.

His hot breath was in her ear. "Don't make a sound. Understand me? Or you'll wish you hadn't."

She nodded, as much as his hand allowed her freedom to move her head.

He moved his hand away from her mouth.

Her arms ached like they had been yanked out of their sockets.

He was fumbling with something, probably rope to bind her. She concentrated on the feel of his hands around her arms. The moment she felt the slightest release, she dashed off like a rabbit, breaking his hold. She hurtled through the woods, picking up her skirts, not knowing if she was running in the right direction. The moon provided barely enough light to cast shadows warning her a mere second before trees loomed in her way.

Dillon's curses came from behind. He was gaining on her.

Her foot hit something solid, and she went down, barely getting her hands in front of her. Pine needles and decayed wood scratched her face and hands and enveloped her with their dying scent. She swept them aside, leaving a wide mark that she'd been there.

He was on top of her the next second, his knee into her back.

"Josh! Help! Help me! Help—" A dirty wad of fabric was shoved in her mouth, cutting off her cries. She pushed it forward with her tongue so it wouldn't gag her, but he quickly fastened it to her head, grabbing some of her hair as he knotted it.

Her hands were bound, and he yanked her up by her arms. Surely they were only hanging on by sinews at this point.

He marched her back the way they came. "I've spent too much time trying to get you alone to let it go to waste. Try anything else, and it'll go much worse next time. Much worse."

She believed him. The gag cut into the corners of her mouth and the rough hemp rope was abrading her wrists. The man's toilet water—just like on the ferry—was overwhelming. Being forced to breathe through her nose meant there was no avoiding the smell. She fought down the nausea, knowing it would only choke her.

For now, she had to concentrate on leaving as good of a trail as she could for Josh to follow. Not easy to do without the use of her hands. Or Dillon noticing.

She scuffed her feet as he goaded her along, overturning

rocks and twigs. Ruining her shoes in the process, but that wasn't important. When she could, she veered into the underbrush trying to snap off branches. Anything she could get away with. Hoping Dillon just thought she was clumsy.

Because if he figured out what she was doing, her problems were only beginning.

JOSH COULDN'T FIND Emily anywhere, and no one had seen her. Unease shaped into a hard ball and rose in his chest. The band had stopped playing, the booths were packing up, and folks were headed home. Emily wouldn't have left without telling him. She'd been good about not going anywhere alone. And even if something had upset her, he couldn't see her taking off. This had been her night. She would have said something to Maggie or Becca.

He grabbed Seth's shoulder as he was helping Maggie and Becca pack up one of the food booths. "Can I talk to you for a minute?" He nodded toward the schoolhouse.

"Sure." Seth's long strides matched Josh's, his brow furrowed. "What is it?"

"Emily's missing. Nobody's seen her. She wouldn't go off on her own. I'm thinking Dillon or Dawson's gang got her somehow. We've got to find her."

Seth's eyes hardened. He gave a quick nod. "Okay. Let's round up some help and some lanterns and see what we can find." He moved off, hailing James and Sy.

Josh's stomach filled with lead. He and Seth had been friends long enough that neither of them had to say it. Finding Emily in the dark was going to be very difficult and would require some divine intervention. He shot up a prayer and then hurried off after Seth.

Chapter Twenty-Six

The first haze of dawn woke Emily. She was stiff, sore, and disoriented. By the rough feel against her back, she must be sitting against a tree. She was in a clearing with the remains of a fire. Two horses nickered nearby. Dillon slept near the cold fire ring. When he never lit it last night, she knew her chances of being found quickly were dim.

The sound of breaking branches and footsteps through the woods shot hope through her heart. Josh had found her and was coming to rescue her. With the gag in her mouth, she couldn't even cry out, but she tried, her squeals and groans going no further than her feet.

She studied the woods in the direction of the sounds, waiting for Josh to make his appearance so this nightmare could be over. The few noises she could make seemed to have no effect on Dillon, and she prayed he would stay asleep. She didn't want him to pull a gun on Josh, and Josh wasn't normally armed.

The sound got closer. A figure moved beyond the branches. A man. Her gaze darted to Dillon but he was still asleep.

The man ducked a branch and stepped into the clearing.

It wasn't Josh.

It was... Dillon?

Disappointment and confusion warred within her chest. Was she delusional? She hadn't remembered hitting her head.

The man spotted her, and his face clouded with anger. He strode toward her. "Are you okay? Did he hurt you?"

She couldn't answer; she just stared at him. He looked just like Dillon, but he was dressed differently, and he didn't wear that awful scent.

Twins.

This was the man who had grabbed her outside the boardinghouse, but he hadn't kidnapped her or hurt her the way Dillon had.

The man moved over to Dillon and roughly shook him. "Dillon! What have you done? Wake up!"

Dillon moaned and rolled over. "Leave me alone, McKay. You couldn't fix it your way, so now we do it my way. If Dawson doesn't get that money, we're all dead anyway."

McKay. So that was the other one's name. Funny, he hadn't been on the wanted poster, though if no one knew they were twins, both of them could commit crimes with only one of them being blamed for it.

McKay rubbed his hands over his face. "Why don't you make us some breakfast? I'll see to the girl."

He walked over to her and squatted. "I'm sorry for what my brother did. He's always causing trouble, and I'm always trying to get him out of it. This was supposed to be the last time. I'm going to take the gag out of your mouth and untie you. But please don't run off. We're in the middle of nowhere, and you'd get lost and hurt." He lowered his voice. "I'm going to get you back home, but I need your help with the money."

He untied the gag and removed it.

She tried to talk, but her mouth was so dry that she only croaked.

McKay turned around. "Any coffee yet, Dillon?"

Dillon hunched over the fire mumbling something. He

turned, revolver in his hand. "Don't try anything, Missy. I'll shoot you dead before you take two steps."

"Let me untie you, and I'll get you some water. But don't try to stand up. Just move your arms and legs a bit to get the feeling back in them." McKay left and came back with a canteen.

She tried to rub the feeling back into her limbs, but they might as well have been wood. McKay held the canteen so she could sip from it, but most of it ended up down the front of her dress. Her now-ruined dress, torn and soiled.

Once Mrs. Parsons learned of this, there would be no school-teacher job for her, even if it meant the school sat empty. Emily was so far from their proper ideal. Maybe Mrs. Parsons and all the other people in Emily's past were right. She wasn't a proper lady and never would be. Her upbringing saw to that. And while her current situation wasn't her fault, things like this happened to people like her.

"Feeling any better?" McKay sat next to her.

"A little. Given the circumstances."

"All we need to know is where the money is. Just tell us, and we'll let you go."

"You're the ones that stole it from the bank?"

"Dillon did. It was a job for the Dawson Gang. I didn't find out about it until later when he told me he'd put the money in your bag on the ferry. He'd panicked. And Dawson was going to kill him if he didn't come up with the money. But then you hid it someplace. I thought if Dillon turned the money in, the marshal would arrest the Dawson Gang and Dillon would be safe. He promised to turn his life around. And if he didn't—" he stared at the ground— "he'd no longer be my brother."

"So who ransacked the boardinghouse? And the Oregon Express office? And hit Josiah over the head?"

McKay stood and went to the fire and dished up whatever Dillon had cooked. He brought back a plate of beans, some hardtack, and a cup of coffee and handed them to Emily.

Her hands, though they felt on fire, now worked well

enough to eat. She would take advantage of the food while she could.

"I'm not proud of it, but I did go through the boarding-house and barn looking for the money. I thought it would be easy to find. And I didn't mean to scare you when I grabbed you. I just wanted this all over and done with."

"And Josiah?" She stared at him.

"Dillon got carried away and reacted badly when Josiah came downstairs and caught us going through his storeroom. Look, I'm not innocent here either. Things got out of hand." He met her stare. "Really out of hand. So where's the money? Let's just get this whole thing over with."

"I don't have it." She finished the beans and dunked the hardtack in the coffee letting it soften so she could take a bite without breaking a tooth. She'd eaten many meals just like this with Silas. "Josh found where I had hidden it in the barn."

She didn't like either of these men, but if she was honest, McKay hadn't acted too differently than she had when she thought Silas had stolen the money. They both were trying to help loved ones, but not in the right way. Funny how that was easier to see in someone else. True, she hadn't physically hurt anyone, but she had hurt Josh by lying to him. Something she'd never do again if she ever saw him.

"We turned it into the sheriff. He knows it's from the Dawson Gang robbery and wired the Portland marshal. I'm assuming the marshal has it now. Or it's been returned to the bank."

McKay's face paled.

IF JOSH HAD SLEPT A WINK, it was because he'd dozed off briefly. His mind wouldn't shut down from thinking about where Emily could be and what danger she could be in. And how he could find her.

The previous night, he and Seth and Mike Riley had looked for a trail. But close to the school there had been too many people and too many footprints. He had to spiral out and then it was too dark.

Just as there was a hint that the sky would soon lighten, Josh was up. Maggie made coffee and breakfast for whoever would eat. It was agreed the boardinghouse would serve as the central station for communications. James and Pa would go back and forth with messages between the search area and the boardinghouse if anyone turned up anything. No one would be in church today. Instead, they'd all be out looking for Emily.

Josh had packed his horse with supplies and was heading out of the barn when Seth and Mike Riley rode up. Pastor Adams joined them. They headed over to the schoolhouse.

He retraced his steps from last night, picturing the harvest festival and where he'd last seen Emily. If something had upset her, she might have gone around to the far side of the school-house to compose herself. Where it was dark.

He started there.

A tuft of grass kicked up, not tramped down as would be expected. He sighted a line to the woods from there and started walking.

EMILY'S MIND spun as the two men hunched over the fire, their voices low, one argumentative, one urgent and pleading. Wasn't too hard to figure out which was which. How could two brothers—twins even—be so different?

Dillon hadn't turned his back to her completely, and he kept glancing over, his revolver pointed at her. Even though she was no longer tied up, he'd shoot her before she could get to her leaden feet. McKay's words came back to her. She didn't even know where she was. She might get out of this danger only to find herself hopelessly lost in the woods, running away from safety instead of to it. She'd have to wait for an opening.

Her mind drifted to the folks from the boardinghouse. Josh would be out looking for her, along with the other men. Her best chance was to let Josh come to her. She hoped she'd left enough of a trail for him to follow.

Her heart softened at the thought of him. She reached up and found the locket still around her neck. Tears of gratitude welled in her eyes that it hadn't broken during Dillon's rough handling of her. She fingered the cool metal. She had no doubt he'd search for her. He knew who she really was.

And so did Maggie and Mrs. Luke and Becca. And they were the only people whose opinions mattered. Mrs. Parsons and those other townspeople didn't know her. And while it stung that she might never be considered a proper lady, in the big scheme of things, did it truly matter what they thought? Sure, she'd lose a job she truly loved. But she could work for Maggie and the stage line. Maybe Mrs. Luke was right. She should stay and build on what she had begun instead of starting over. She didn't have to return to Portland. She had a new life here, and running away—for once—felt like the wrong choice.

McKay and Dillon got to their feet. McKay's face darkened, and he strode to her. "I'm sure you need to make a stop in the woods before we go." He hauled her to her feet.

"Be quick about it." Dillon hauled his saddle to the horse. "We've been in one place too long as it is."

McKay roughly pulled her along to the woods. She did need to make a stop, though not with him watching. But she knew that look. He had a plan.

"Listen, we don't have much time." They came to a halt far enough away that Dillon couldn't hear McKay's whispered words. "He's not too happy about the money. But he figures Dawson would be pleased to take you instead."

Her limbs turned to water, and she grabbed a tree for support. She could only imagine what life with Dawson would be like. She'd been skirting that kind of life and those kind of men her whole life. She'd rather die. And a few times she thought she might. Silas had protected her. She had to thank him for that.

Her gaze darted around. How could she make an escape? Where could she go? She knew one thing: She wasn't going to let Dillon turn her over to Dawson. If he killed her as she tried to escape, it was a better alternative.

McKay grabbed her arm. "Don't run off now. I'm going to try to distract him or restrain him in some way. You'll know it when you see it. Make sure you run in that direction." He pointed to the opposite side of where they'd made camp. "It'll take you to the stage road that leads to Reedsville."

She met his gaze. "Thank you, McKay. I know it's hard to have a loved one who makes bad choices. I hope you'll be able to find some peace."

He nodded. "I hope so too. If I can get Dillon to California, we might be shed of all this trouble and be able to start a new life. We'd best get back."

Chapter Twenty-Seven

J osh! Over here!"

Josh turned.

James crashed through the woods waving a piece of paper. "It's for the sheriff. A telegram." James panted out the words and handed the page to Mike Riley.

Riley read it then looked up, his mouth a tight line. "The marshal's response to my telegram of last night. Dawson's gang is believed to still be in the Portland area. The marshal thinks Emily has run off to be with them."

Josh shook his head. "People get something stuck in their mind, and they see only what they want to see. He wouldn't be any help anyway."

Riley nodded. "I was hoping he'd let us use some of that money as bait if we needed to."

"We've got a good enough trail to follow. Either they were dragging her through the woods, or she made sure to leave marks I could find. She's a smart woman. We just have to find her before any harm comes to her."

He told James roughly where he thought they'd be headed in case there was any news. Then they moved deeper into the woods.

Gaze scanning for the next clue, his mind flowed freely, cycling through images of Emily. She'd become such a part of his life, he couldn't imagine her not in it. Failing to find her was not an option.

While he couldn't help but wish she had trusted him with the whole story sooner, he understood now why she hadn't. And if she could be so loyal to a man like Silas, how much more so would she be to him, a man who only wanted to be nothing but good to her? For the rest of her life, he wanted her to feel cherished and protected and never afraid to share her thoughts with him.

While the Parsonses might not see her as worthy of being their schoolteacher, he thought there was no one finer to teach the town's children. With her perseverance, loyalty, and kindness, she'd made strong friends with Maggie and Becca. And he knew those women well enough to know their protective instincts. Emily could have no better friends on her side.

He stopped and searched for the next clue. He spotted a broken branch up ahead. They had been continuing in a fairly straight line, headed generally for the hills above where the mudslide had cut across the road. He hadn't been up in those hills since then, but it would be a fair place to make camp. Close to escape routes but away from prying eyes.

He prayed they got there in time.

WITHOUT LOOKING like she was doing so, Emily studied the men as they packed up the horses. She knew right where she wanted to dart when she had an opening. North, not west. She didn't want to give away that she knew the direction of the road. She could angle that way through dense brush and trees, making it difficult, if not impossible, for them to follow on horseback.

She had a plan. Now she needed an opening.

"Listen, Dillon. I don't want to meet Red Dawson. I don't

want to be part of his gang. Let's just head to California. The gold mines aren't all played out. And even if they are, there are plenty of other opportunities for us down there. We can start over, and no one will know where we are."

Dillon grabbed McKay's shirt. "Sounds like you don't know the meaning of loyalty. I told Red I could be trusted with that money. He's been plenty patient with me. Now if I don't show up with that girl tomorrow, I might as well shoot myself in the head. Because Red will be eager to do it, and there won't be any place far enough from him. A man's word's gotta mean something." He gave McKay a final shake before letting him go.

"Dillon, you've got your head so messed up, you're turning things around. A man don't owe no loyalty to an outlaw like Red. If you can save your own skin, you oughta do it. Plus, what about me? What about loyalty to your family? I've put my neck out for you, and I don't want no part of this."

"Then walk away, McKay. Just walk away."

"I can't do that." His fist connected hard and fast with Dillon's jaw.

Dillon staggered back, his horse shying away, but he didn't fall.

Emily gathered her feet under her, ready to spring. Willing her sore body to move quickly when it needed to and refusing to think of the alternative.

He rushed McKay, grabbing him around the waist and tackling him to the ground.

She didn't wait to see what happened next. As quietly as she could, she bounded out of the camp and into the woods, her eyes focused on the next tree branch to duck or the next log to clamber over. She could hear a commotion and shouting behind her, but if the men were fighting or coming after her, she didn't turn to find out.

Lord, help me discover the road!

AN ODD SENSATION prickled at the base of Josh's neck. One he never ignored. He scanned the area but couldn't find the reason for it.

"Riley, I have an idea." He slid off his horse. "You keep heading this way. If you don't stumble across their camp, you'll hit the road between Portland and Reedsville. I'm going to cut through and head over there and meet you that way. If they are in a hurry and decide to take the road, I'll have a better chance of seeing them."

Riley nodded. "Three shots if you find anything."

"You too." He led his horse through the brush and down the embankment to the road before remounting. He could make better time this way. He couldn't shake the feeling that they wouldn't be hanging around camp. Especially if they were supposed to meet up with Dawson. A cold chill slunk through his body at the thought of what a man like Dawson would do to Emily.

He had to find her first.

Kicking his horse to a canter, he topped the rise. He rubbed his eyes. Surely his wishful thinking was making him see things.

Emily was sliding down the embankment just past the mudslide.

He spurred his horse toward her.

Her head turned at the sound of the hoofbeats, a panicked look on her face. Oh Emily! He hoped he never saw that again. Then he was upon her, pulling her into the saddle in front of him, holding her tight, relief weakening him.

"Are you okay? Anything hurt?"

She nodded and then shook her head. "I'm okay. They're back in the woods. Or they were." She pointed.

"Plug your ears." He lifted his revolver from its holster and fired into the air three times. "That will either bring them or Mike Riley running." His gaze scanned the woods and the road ahead. He squeezed her. "You're safe now. It's going to be okay."

She turned with a warm gaze full of promise. "I know. I knew you would find me." She trembled in his arms.

A crashing through the woods alerted him, and he shifted his revolver's aim. Mike Riley appeared. Josh lowered his gun.

He bent his mouth next to her ear. "And I'm never going to let you go."

Chapter Twenty-Eight

A knock sounded on Emily's door, and she startled. It had been nearly a week since she'd been taken by Dillon, but she was still a bit jumpy when something caught her off guard.

She opened the door.

Maggie stood there with a dress draped over her arm. "Put this on with your best hat and meet me downstairs."

She took the dress and frowned. "Where did this come from?" It was a lovely pink-striped dimity, with delicate lace at the throat and cuffs. She had seen one just like it in Fulton's.

Maggie gave a soft smile and tilted her head. "Josh. Now, no more questions. Just do yourself up pretty and come downstairs." She pulled the door shut, and her footsteps retreated.

A thousand questions flew through Emily's head. She couldn't help the smile at the thought of Josh. He'd been so thoughtful this week, spending every spare moment with her that he could.

An emergency school board meeting had been called where the teacher they had hired, a Miss Spencer, gave them what-for over their "dishonest and misleading" advertisement. She was on the stage the next day. The rest of the meeting dissolved into arguments and discussions that fell into two camps: those who thought Emily should be dismissed and school closed until a suitable teacher could be found and those who thought she was brave and a wonderful example to the children.

Emily herself had stayed home, not wanting to witness her character being assassinated. But she hadn't been anxious about the outcome. She had the "peace that passeth all understanding." Her past wasn't much of a secret anymore, and there were still people who loved her. A burden had been lifted, and she had never felt so light and free.

Sheriff Riley had shown up at the boardinghouse after the meeting. He had no news about the Dawson Gang or the Rogers brothers. But he did have news that she was still the teacher in Reedsville.

Emily stopped woolgathering and donned the dress. It fit her surprisingly well. The extra lace allowed the sleeves to cover her long arms and the flounces made the dress the right length.

Yes, it had been an unusual week, to say the least. While she had the teaching job, she insisted that the teacher's cottage go to Pastor Adams. Maggie had, of course, welcomed her to stay at the boardinghouse.

She pinned on her hat and checked her reflection in the mirror over the washstand. Where was Josh? She hadn't seen him all day. She would have to find and thank him.

She moved lightly down the stairs and entered the parlor. What she saw stopped her in her tracks.

Ladies from the town, dressed in their best, filled the room. A small table had been placed in the middle of the parlor, covered with a lacy tablecloth and a silver tea set with dainty china cups and plates of cookies and cakes.

Maggie stepped forward. "Welcome to our first Reedsville Ladies Tea. Won't you join us?"

The women stood and applauded, their gloves muting the clapping.

Tears pricked her eyes, and she blinked them back. How did Maggie know? And then she knew. Josh. She truly did have a lot to thank him for. She put on a full, genuine smile and moved forward to greet the ladies of this town.

Her town.

Soon the soft sounds of laughter and women's voices floated around her as she sipped tea and nibbled on a cookie from her spot next to Becca.

"While Josh mentioned the idea," Becca whispered to her, "I think the credit belongs to you. Something like this has been long overdue. We need to make it a regular tradition, and I think you should organize it. Think of all the good a ladies society could do for the town."

Warmth spread through her chest at the thought. Someone thought she could do good for the town.

Why, yes. Yes, she could.

WHEN THE LAST of the ladies departed Maggie's parlor, Josh made his way out of the barn. He and Pa had converted part of it to a woodworking shop. It gave Pa something to do, and it was a good hedge against the day the railroad would make its way here, if the rumors were to be believed.

Truth be told, he'd had a hard time keeping his mind on his work. After making two wrong cuts, he'd resorted to organizing the wood and supplies and letting Pa do the actual cutting.

He headed to the cabin, washed up, and put on a clean shirt. Striding to the front of the boardinghouse, he knocked on the door, feeling a bit silly but knowing it was the right thing to do. He twirled his hat in his hands.

Emily opened the door. Her eyes widened, then a smile danced across her face. "Josh! Why did you knock? And why did you use this door?" She opened the door wider and stepped back. She was wearing the dress he'd gotten her, the pink of the dress matching the pink in her cheeks. The locket he'd given her nestled in the lace on the front. Pleasure coursed through him, and he wondered how many more things he could give her.

He stepped into the parlor. "It's what a man does when he comes calling on a lady he's courting." He took her hand. "And that's what I intend to do. Emily Stanton, do I have your permission to court you?"

She covered her mouth, and she nodded. She lowered her hand. "Um, yes." A smile broke out across her face. "Yes, I would be honored to have you court me."

He slipped his hand around her waist and pulled her to him. He lowered his head and touched his lips to hers, conveying all the promise and the future he hoped to have with her.

When he pulled back, he gazed at her pale gray eyes. "Just don't expect this courting to go on for too long." He grinned and gave her a wink.

She returned his grin. And then she reached up and placed her hand over his cheek before tilting her face to return his kiss.

What's next?

What other adventures await the folks of Reedsville?

Does Josh propose to Emily?

What happens with Maggie and Pastor Roy?

Find out by going to https://jennifercrosswhite.com/Maggie to get "Maggie and the Preacher: a Route Home short story."

You'll also get my latest news and updates at and the prequel novella, *Be Mine*.

My bimonthly updates include upcoming books written by me and other authors you will enjoy, information on all my latest releases, sneak peeks of yet-to-be-released chapters, and exclusive giveaways. Your email address will never be shared, and you can unsubscribe at any time.

If you enjoyed this book, please consider leaving a review. Reviews can be as simple as "I couldn't put it down. I can't wait for the next one" and help raise the author's visibility and lets other readers find her.

Keep reading for a sneak peak of *Finally Home*, the last book in The Route Home series.

Acknowledgments

This book would not be possible without the patience and willingness to read many, many drafts by Diana Brandmeyer, Liz Tolsma, and Danielle Reid. Special thanks to Sara Benner for her expert proofreading and Pamela Martinez for her eagle eye! Many thanks to my beta readers!

Much thanks and love to my children, Caitlyn Elizabeth and Joshua Alexander, for supporting my dream for many years and giving me time to write. And to my Lord Jesus Christ for giving me the ability to live out my dreams and directing my paths.

Author's Note

The 1880s was a fascinating time in American history. The country was recovering from its greatest wounding, the Civil War. People were moving West to make new lives for themselves. Progress, in the form of trains, telegraphs, gas, and electricity were making life easier, and new inventions were just around the corner. Out West in particular, women were becoming more independent and taking charge of their own lives, including careers and schooling.

I chose to set this story in Oregon, because I visited there on a trip in high school and fell in love with its beauty. The very kernel of this story started as an AP English project that year. The characters never left me alone and over the years the story grew, morphed, and changed as my writing skills developed. Reedsville is inspired by the real town of Molalla, Oregon, which was the end of the trail and the beginning of a new life for many pioneers of the time.

I enjoyed watching as my characters adapted to the changes of their time, drawing on their strength, love, and community to continue to thrive and make a life for themselves.

I hope you have enjoyed this trip back in time as much as I have.

About the Author

My favorite thing is discovering how much there is to love about America the Beautiful and the great outdoors. I'm an Amazon bestselling author, a mom to two navigating the young adult years while battling my daughter's juvenile arthritis, exploring the delights of my son's autism, and keeping gluten free.

A California native who's spent significant time in the Midwest, I'm thrilled to be back in the Golden State. Follow me on social media to see all my adventures and how I get inspired for my books!

www.JLCrosswhite.com
    Twitter: @jenlcross
    Facebook: Author Jennifer Crosswhite

Instagram: jencrosswhite
Pinterest: Tandem Services

facebook.com/authorjennifercrosswhite
twitter.com/jenlcross
instagram.com/jencrosswhite
pinterest.com/tandemservices

Preview of *Finally Home*, Book 3 of The Route Home series.

~1882, PORTLAND, OREGON

Amelia Martin clapped her gloved hands together before glancing at her father and noticing his scowl. She shoved them behind her back. Still, she couldn't help but rock forward on the pointed toes of her kidskin boots. As they stood in front of the Oregon Express office in Portland, the shiny red stagecoach pulled in front of them. And Josh Benson was driving. She'd know him anywhere from his description in the letters Mrs. Kincaid—wait, she was Mrs. Adams now— had sent them. That dark curly hair. She couldn't see his dimples, as he wasn't smiling. But she'd bet a cutting of her mother's prized blush damask rose that they were there.

He would be marrying the town's schoolteacher, Miss Emily Stanton. So romantic! She hoped she and Father would be invited to the wedding. She just loved weddings. And since schoolteachers couldn't be married, Amelia planned to take the position Miss Stanton currently held. The town had offered it to her. Father hadn't given his blessing yet, but he would.

She slid her arm through Father's. "Aren't you excited for this adventure?"

He patted her hand, a slight smile flitting across his face, barely visible under his neatly trimmed mustache and beard, but not reaching his eyes. It never did anymore. "I'll be happy when we're settled in our new place. There's much that needs to be done before then."

True. And it had been a lengthy journey from upstate New York to Chicago by train, and then another train through some of the most diverse and spectacular scenery of prairies, deserts, and mountains. In Sacramento, California, they switched to the Oregon and California train for the final leg of their journey to Portland. And somehow her cuttings had survived the entire journey. As tired as she was, excitement coursed through her.

The end was so near. And she would get to ride a stagecoach! Just like in her favorite dime novels.

An older man and a younger one loaded their valises and trunks into the boot. And most importantly, her cuttings, wrapped in burlap and nestled in damp sawdust that she refreshed each night. They were her mother's legacy, and they meant more to her than anything else she owned.

Their household goods would be coming by freighter at some point. And because of the dime novels she read, she knew all the correct terms for life in the West and what they meant. Her latest novel was safely tucked in the emerald-green velvet reticule that swung from her wrist. Oh, she was living out a proper adventure, just like in one of her books! The only thing that would make this perfect would be if Mother were with them. She swallowed down the thought. No tears, or even the hint of them, would mar this adventure. She brushed her hands over her deep-green wool coat that matched her traveling suit, picking at a speck of dust.

Josh Benson nodded in their direction as footsteps came up behind them. Amelia tore her gaze away from the stagecoach. A man had joined them. He was sharply dressed in a dark suit and crisp white shirt. Taller than her father and possibly a little older than herself, he was lean with shoulders that filled out his suit coat. He smiled and tipped his hat at her, his golden-brown eyes —such an unusual color—twinkling. "Miss." He turned to include her father. "Are you folks traveling all the way to Reedsville?"

Father nodded. "We are. How about you, Mr.—?"

"Hank Paulson." He stuck out his hand and shook Father's. "I've been living there for a while now. It's a friendly town, good people. You'll like it there, I believe."

"Dr. Luke Martin and my daughter, Amelia. I've taken the position of town physician. We're relocating from New York."

"The town is surely in need of a doctor."

This man would be on the stage with them. All the questions

she could ask him about the town raced through her brain. "Mrs. Adams has been writing to us about Reedsville and the people. We'll be staying in her boardinghouse until our house is built. I can't wait to get there."

He smiled. "You won't have to wait long. Josh is ready for us. Shall we?" He swept his hand toward the open stagecoach door.

Amelia stepped on the small box, and with Mr. Benson's assistance, entered the stagecoach.

He flashed her a smile, and those dimples appeared.

She grinned in triumph as she took her seat. Father sat next to her and Mr. Paulson across from them. The rest of the stagecoach filled with passengers, making for a tight fit. She kept her skirts firmly tucked under to keep them from brushing against Mr. Paulson.

Soon they were off. The jostling made it necessary for her to grip the seat, but the scenery that passed the window was breathtaking. So many variations of green! Back in New York, everything was still under layers of snow, the trees only bare sticks. Here it looked like it was nearly spring, even though it was only the end of January. Even the cool air had a hint of warmth to it.

Between the scenery, the jostling, and the noise, Amelia didn't ask any questions of Mr. Paulson. She'd discover it all as she experienced it.

A sharp report split the air. The coach jerked, and shouts came from outside. She caught Mr. Paulson's gaze. His brow furrowed, and he leaned to peer out. He reached inside his jacket and pulled out an envelope. He nodded at Father. "Any valuables, best try to hide them. We're being held up."

Robbed? Oh this was just like one of her books. Except she wouldn't swoon like the heroines often did. That was silly, frankly. She whispered a quick prayer for safety.

Mr. Paulson shoved the envelope in the seat cushion behind him then pointed to her reticule. "Anything in there you want me to try to hide?"

"Oh no. Merely a handkerchief and a book." But her hand

went to her neck. Her mother's cameo, one of the few things she was allowed to keep for their journey West. It had a gold setting and chain, so it was worth some money, but of far greater value was its sentimental one. She tucked it into her dress, her high collar hiding the chain.

Father's arm came around her shoulders, pulling her close.

The stagecoach slowed to a stop, and horsemen replaced the woods as the scenery out the window.

Mr. Paulson cut his voice low. "Just do as they say. They likely want the strongbox and any valuables. But generally no one gets hurt, and they'll let us on our way once they get what they want."

A man on horseback with a bandana over his face bent to scout out the inside of the stagecoach. "No funny stuff, ya hear? Get on out here, and bring your valuables with you."

The stagecoach door flew open, another masked man holding it. "Don't none of you men try to be brave, or you'll get shot for your trouble."

Amelia trembled. While this was like something out of one of her dime novels, it might be a bit more adventure than she'd like.

What had they gotten into?

Hank followed Amelia Martin out of the stagecoach. He couldn't help but notice her comely form, the green coat that highlighted her eyes, or the sun glinting off her reddish-brown hair. He'd been hoping this stagecoach ride would be enjoyable. It was not to be.

He kept to the side and in front of her, her father flanking the other side. What a way to be introduced to their new town. He scanned the robbers for any sign that might help Sheriff Riley identify them or their horses. One horse, a paint, resembled Tim Donnally's that had been stolen last week. So horse thieves too. The men were dirty and scruffy enough that he wasn't sure he could even identify his own brother if he were one of them. Not that Philip would ever be dirty or scruffy.

The final passengers exited the coach. He studied the men. He didn't know any of them, and he hoped no one would try to be a hero. They were evenly matched numbers-wise with the robbers, but the robbers all had their hands firmly on their firearms. Josh had been forced to surrender his shotgun.

The man who had opened the stagecoach door went around to each passenger collecting their valuables, patting the men's pockets to make sure no one was hiding anything. Another two were rummaging in the boot.

And the ringleader had his shotgun pointed at Josh. "Go ahead and toss down that strongbox I know you have up in that so-called secret driver's compartment."

Josh moved slowly, deliberately, but he complied.

The robber stealing from the passengers reached Hank and the Martins. "Easy now. Give me your wallet." His gun shifted to Miss Martin. Hank stiffened and shifted his weight closer to her. "And you, missy, hand over any jewelry and that fancy bag of yours."

Miss Martin paled. A faint sprinkling of freckles stood out across her nose and cheeks. He'd be enchanted in any other circumstance.

"I'm wearing no jewelry. And there's nothing of value in my reticule. See?" She opened the drawstring pouch and held it toward him.

The man raked his gaze up and down her form. Hank wanted to punch him. Based on the slight movement Dr. Martin made and Miss Martin's restraining squeeze on his arm, Hank suspected he wasn't alone in that sentiment.

The robber grabbed the bag and dumped it into his hand. A scrap of lacy linen and a dime novel fell out. She hadn't been lying about her lack of valuables, thank goodness.

The man scowled. "A book? I ain't got no use for reading."

He tossed the bag and its contents to the ground then chuckled. "But I might come back for a different kind of payment."

Over my dead body.

A scuffle at the boot caught Hank's attention. Items flew out the back, including some burlap sacks that broke open and scattered sawdust and plant material over the ground. What on earth was that?

Miss Martin whimpered.

He turned to see her gaze on the sacks, her gloved hand at her lips. They must be her items. But what they were, he had no idea. Her face crumpled, and she blinked rapidly. The encounter with the robber must have upset her more than she let on.

One of the passengers lunged for the robber. Looked like Bill Benchly, a saloon owner. Two others joined in.

Hank snatched Miss Martin about the waist and rolled her under the stagecoach.

The other robbers leaped in and a melee ensued. In the midst of the wrestling match, a gun went off. The shouts and several other gunshots faded from his awareness as the blackness pressed in. *Lord, please. Not now.* Reciting the Twenty-Third Psalm in his head, he deliberately steadied his breath and opened his eyes, which he hadn't realized he'd closed. He could see daylight. The space wasn't that tight. Slowly the blackness receded.

He became aware of Miss Martin's form pressed beneath him. Small and soft. He forced his mind away from those thoughts. She would likely be upset that he had dirtied her dress.

She struggled under him, trying to push him off. The scent of lilacs filled his nose.

"Shh, it's not safe."

She whispered something he couldn't hear over the commotion.

Horses whinnied. Men shouted. Hoofbeats started then receded.

He peeked out from under the stagecoach. Dr. Martin bent over a man. A woman knelt next to him, sobbing.

An elbow to Hank's ribs elicited a grunt, and he rolled over.

Miss Martin shimmied out from the stagecoach and ran— not to her father—but to the burlap sacks.

Hank slid out from under the stagecoach, fast on her heels.

She reached the first sack, scraping the sawdust and plants back into the bag.

Plants?

She glanced back at him. "Help me." Then she began coughing.

Dr. Martin jerked his head in her direction, frowned, and returned attending to his patient.

"What are these?" Hank studied what appeared to be a stick in his hand. Some others had a bit of greenery on them. Odd.

"My cuttings. The only thing I have left from my mother. They can't dry out. Pack the damp sawdust back around their roots and put them back in the burlap."

He did as she asked, taking in the scene around him as he worked. One man had been shot, the one Doc was working on. The rest seemed no worse for wear, picking up their hats, dusting themselves off, and repacking bags the robbers had strewn over the ground.

Josh gave directions and tended to the horses.

Hank packed the last burlap bag and handed it into the boot.

Miss Martin continued coughing.

"Are you all right?" Perhaps Josh had a canteen if she needed a drink.

"I'm coughing because you pushed my face into the dust and wouldn't let me breathe."

Oh. He'd tried to be a hero and had, once again, failed miserably. At least she'd only inhaled a bit of dust.

She rummaged through her father's doctor bag and came up with a small vial, which she opened and placed under her nose.

They loaded the injured man onto the stagecoach. It was Benchly. Some of the men rode up top to make room for him to lie down inside. Miss Martin followed her father onto the coach, carrying his medical bag.

But she didn't glance his way once.

Her reticule lay in the dirt where the robber had tossed it. Hank picked it up and dusted it off. She'd likely want it back. He snatched up her handkerchief and her book as well. *Her Love or Her Life*. The cover promised adventure and romance. Maybe today's adventure was a bit more than Miss Martin had encountered in the pages of this book. Maybe she'd learned that a hero only existed there and not in real life. Thank God He had kept them safe.

He tucked it all into his coat pocket and scrambled up next to Josh once all the other passengers were settled. He told himself Josh could use another set of eyes for the remainder of the trip home.

But the truth was, he didn't want to be near Miss Martin. He'd never felt less like a hero.

Buy it now! Click here.

Books by Jennifer Crosswhite

Contemporary Romance

The Inn at Cherry Blossom Lane

Can the summer magic of Lake Michigan bring first loves back together? Or will the secret they discover threaten everything they love?

Historical Romance

The Route Home Series

Be Mine

A woman searching for independence. A man searching for education. Can a simple thank you note turn into something more?

Coming Home

He was why she left. Now she's falling for him. Can a woman who turned her back on her hometown come home to find justice for her brother without falling in love with his best friend?

The Road Home

He is a stagecoach driver just trying to do his job. She is returning to her suitor only to find he has died. When a stack of stolen money shows up in her bag, she thinks the past she has desperately tried to hide has come back to haunt her.

Finally Home

The son of a wealthy banker, Hank Paulson poses as a lumberjack to carve out his own identity. But in a stagecoach robbery gone wrong, he meets Amelia Martin, a a soon-to-be schoolteacher with a vivid imagination, a gift for making things grow, and an obsession with dime novels. As the town is threatened by a past enemy, Hank might just be the hero they all need. Can he help without revealing who he is? And will Amelia love him when she learns the truth?

Books by JL Crosswhite

Romantic Suspense

The Hometown Heroes Series

Promise Me

Cait can't catch a break. What she witnessed could cost her job and her beloved farmhouse. Will Greyson help her or only make things worse?

Protective Custody

She's a key witness in a crime shaking the roots of the town's power brokers. He's protecting a woman he'll risk everything for. Doing the right thing may cost her everything. Including her life.

Flash Point

She's a directionally-challenged architect who stumbled on a crime that could destroy her life's work. He's a firefighter protecting his hometown… and the woman he loves.

Special Assignment

A brain-injured Navy pilot must work with the woman in charge of the program he blames for his injury. As they both grasp to save their careers, will their growing attraction hinder them as they attempt solve the mystery of who's really at fault before someone else dies?

In the Shadow Series

Off the Map

For her, it's a road trip adventure. For him, it's his best shot to win her back. But for the stalker after her, it's revenge.

Out of Range

It's her chance to prove she's good enough. It's his chance to prove he's more than just a fun guy. Is it their time to find love, or is her secret admirer his deadly competition?

Over Her Head

On a church singles' camping trip that no one wants to be on, a weekend away to renew and refresh becomes anything but. A group of friends trying to find their footing do a good deed and get much more than they bargained for.

Made in the USA
Las Vegas, NV
03 September 2024

94723624R00156